AS ONE WORLD BURNS, CAN A MAN STOP
HIS OWN FROM SLIPPING AWAY?

# SOLAR RAIN

## SEAN M. T. SHANAHAN

# PART 1

## JULY 2189

Riku sagged against the ship's railing and grunted. It was warm—too warm. Predawn in the South Pacific usually chilled him to the bone, and that first cup of tea provided comfort in contrast with the cold beauty of the ocean. The ocean was blanketed in darkness and fog—warm fog.

It was perplexing.

"You're up early, my love." Aya emerged from the cabin and nuzzled into his embrace, rousing him from his contemplations. "It's not usually this warm so early, is it?"

"Never at this time of year. You're up early too," Riku noticed.

She raised a tablet to his face. A bleary-eyed young woman looked back from the screen, and the wrinkles in Riku's face crinkled with joy.

"Father," the young woman bowed to the camera and smiled.

"Hatsue! How is our granddaughter?"

She smirked, "As you can hear behind me, Father, Yasu has been up since early morning, constructing some contraption." She manoeuvred the camera to face a little girl playing on a wooden living room floor behind her. The child was fitting together brightly coloured blocks into a large and intricate structure. "She will be an engineer, I think."

"Surely this isn't why you have called us so early?" Aya chimed in with a smile.

"No, Mother, I think I have wonderful news. I have begun to crave peaches again!" Her smile nearly split her face in two. "We are going to the doctor today."

"This is wonderful news!" Aya cried.

"What? I don't follow," Riku said.

Aya nudged him, "All the women on my side of the family crave peaches when they're pregnant—remember me? Yasu may have a sibling on the way!"

"Ah, this *is* wonderful! Congratulations, Hatsue—you bring us great joy."

"Thank you, Fath . . . ." The screen buzzed and then went dead, displaying a faint connection error icon on the top right corner.

"What happened?" Aya asked.

"The connection went bad, Aya. No matter. We can call later. Until then, the dawn is coming."

The fog around the vessel brightened and bronzed as the heat rose drastically. Aya pulled open her cardigan and fanned at her neck. "This weather isn't right, Riku. What if it affects our results today?"

"It shouldn't; if the deep ocean scanners are affected by a little heat, then we have other problems," he replied.

Beads of sweat formed at their brows. Riku wiped them from his face, grunting again. The radar equipment on the boat above buzzed and fizzled.

"Is that hissing?" Aya asked.

Riku strained his ears. From the approaching dawn, a hissing and bubbling sound approached. It grew louder as the light pierced more fog. The air became humid and ever-increasingly bronze as the minutes passed by.

"It can't be . . . steam?" Riku said.

They locked eyes; the sound grew even louder.

"That can't be right!" Aya cried. "The ocean can't boil!"

"We need to get to the bridge!" Riku's teacup smashed across the deck as they rushed along the walkway and up a steep staircase.

Panting, they entered the bridge cabin, jolting a sleeping figure from resting on a console.

"Helmsman, bring up the latest weather readings!"

"Mmm." The man sleepily typed at the console while he obliviously wiped sweat from his face. His eyes shot wide open. He was fully awake as he exclaimed, "That can't be!"

"What is it?" Aya asked.

"The temperature has increased twenty degrees over the past five minutes!"

"Impossible!" Riku shouted, removing his coat. "Our equipment must be malfunctioning. What do the surrounding weather buoys say?"

"I can't raise any east of us, and the western buoys haven't spiked as much."

Despite the heat, cold dread seeped down Riku's spine. He looked towards the brightening wall of steam, "It's the coming dawn."

"How can that be?" Aya said, her voice strained.

Riku did not answer. "Helmsman, how long until sunrise?"

The helmsman checked his watch and consulted a chart on the rear wall of the bridge. "One minute, sir."

"Sound the alarm! We need to get below deck now!" Riku grabbed Aya by the arm, pulling her outside and down the steep steps as the helmsman sounded the alarm.

The wailing was so sudden, so loud and acute, that they stumbled—they both tumbled onto the deck below, landing in a messed tangle of limbs. Riku shakily pulled himself and Aya upright.

"Are you all right, Aya?" he asked.

But she was looking out to sea.

A titanic wall of white steam rushed towards the vessel like an avalanche out of the haze. Then the boat was hit by the light from the sun as it peeked over the horizon. The light was a bright, searing white beam that pierced through the steam, causing them to cry out and duck under the railing with their skin already blistering.

The boat groaned and creaked as it was super-heated in seconds. Aya and Riku—two old lovers—embraced each other, screaming as a wall of boiling vapour engulfed their scalding bodies.

# PART 2

## FEBRUARY 2222—THIRTY-THREE YEARS LATER

The visual display on my mask's visor wasn't responding quickly enough to my neural interface. The threat tracker was overloaded. There were just too many people to track.

Frustration had me tapping on my visor uselessly, so I directed a call to local Command with the built-in helmet communications link. Minutes passed before Command registered me amongst all the other data noise, but a buzzing connection filled my ears with static . . . eventually.

"This is local Command," the disrupted voice garbled.

"This is Captain Jaysid Moors," I said. "We need to disengage the threat tracker—it's just bogging us down."

"Captain," the voice sighed, creating enough static to make me wince. "Protocol for a situation like this dictates—"

"Protocol is for regular events. The system can't sift through this much data with any use. We're blind out here!"

The static buzzed persistently for a moment.

"Captain Moors, local Command has registered your request and agrees that within your operational area the threat tracker is more detrimental than useful . . ." I rolled my eyes, "Your request is granted. Stay sharp out there."

"I will now." I cancelled the communication.

The threat tracker shut down, and suddenly my neural link could process layouts and unit commands seamlessly without the extra data.

"Thank God!" my comms chirped crisply. An ID tag in the top right of my display read 'Claudin.' "This peace of mind reminds me of my divorce!"

A laughing reply followed quickly from another soldier. "Freedom from getting laid?"

"Let's face it, he wasn't getting laid anyway," a third soldier added.

I smirked briefly but sighed and overrode the squad chatter. "Stow it! I didn't free up our feed just to get bogged down by your incessant chatter. Keep your eyes peeled; we're gonna have to look for threats the old-fashioned way."

"Do you really think anyone will attack Wave One, Captain?" The soldier by me asked over the comms. "I mean, it's literally suicide to stop the colony effort."

"You think they care?" I said solemnly. "These fanatics are mostly young, unskilled people who have no hope of being selected for evacuation. So they flock to gurus who decree God has deemed that we should die and we have no right to deny him . . . you all saw the message they broadcasted. I have a feeling that this fanaticism will make the shelter gang wars look like mere ration riots."

"Fair enough, boss," Claudin said. "What's our plan?"

"Keep roving, scan the crowds, and stay in constant communication. Acknowledge?"

Thirty miniature ID tags blinked at the top right of my display.

"Good."

I let down the interactive map I had been viewing on the overhead display and scanned my surroundings. Crowds of millions lined the multi-tiered chrome platforms as far as the eye could see. The chatter and cheering of the lot drowned out the heavy loading machines and rumblings of Wave One, Colony Ship Four; The Odyssey 2.

I rolled my eyes as I looked at the gargantuan lettering on the grey bulbous leviathan looming above me. The next two waves had three other Odysseys. It seemed as the masses perished over the years, so did our originality. The other four ships of wave one had two Icaruses, one Roamer, and The Star Wanderer. There was an Odyssey 1, but it melted when the shields failed during one of the

Solar Rains . . . along with several thousand builders. The silver lining to that was my wife got an extra half ration for the next few weeks.

But Dad would have been upset. These ships were a wasted opportunity to pick a name more . . . original. Three unoriginally named ships from Wave One, all departing from this launch station today.

In the distance, behind the chrome viewing tiers, the city's bronze spires pierced the red aurora above. Beyond the rolling red lights, a gargantuan object loomed ominously in the sky, extending from horizon to horizon—a rail gun that reached from the moon to the terrestrial asteroid belt. The Space Cannon—as we called it—would magnetically propel the giant colony ships along its track until they reached relativistic speeds and ejected across the stars and towards our new home. The new planet had an official name, but it did not sit well with me. I called it New Terra.

The ground rumbled, and the crowds cheered; in the distance, Icarus 2 rose from the ground atop a cloud of black-grey smog. The ship was a bulky, awkward-looking thing that propelled itself with four gigantic boosters. The crowds below it would be engulfed in the smog.

"We hadn't been briefed on the smoke," a sergeant radioed.

"Luckily, we have our heads-up display, then," a corporal replied.

"Soldiers!" I snapped, "Focus on our own launch pad!"

They were silent as Odyssey 2 rumbled. Its great loading bay doors clanked shut, and the hundreds of passenger gangways were retracting. It was ready; the engines began to quake. The crowds screamed and threw streamers and confetti, which clattered down on my visor like a shower of debris. One streamer got caught in my disruptor field and pirouetted about my shoulders, obscuring my view until I angrily snatched it down. One of the soldiers near me was struggling to remove several such distractions from his disruptor field, too.

The Space Cannon streaked with a sharp, electric blue light in the sky, and the crowds became riotous. The Star Wanderer had launched from the other side of the planet and had entered the Space Cannon first—it was away.

"And humanity is now an interstellar species!" an announcer boomed over the din. "Now, please ready yourselves. Odyssey 2 is about to depart."

The boosters rumbled and sputtered; I knew it would take another few minutes to fire up. I gazed towards Icarus 2 as it rose in the distance, a great angular blob floating in the sky like a failed moon.

The Space Cannon streaked again—Roamer was away.

Then my heart stopped. The rumbling of Odyssey 2 and the roaring crowds went silent—my neural interface scrubbed them from my awareness when my adrenaline spiked.

Five small objects propelled by trails of fire emerged from the black smoke below Icarus 2. The ship carried one million people and hovered over another few million below.

My comms buzzed with dozens of panicked voices.

"Contact! Do you see the contact!?"

"Sweet God!"

"No . . . ."

"What do we do?!"

"Captain?!"

"Can we intercept?!"

But I already knew there was nothing we could do.

The five rockets collided in quick succession, lighting the sky like five miniature suns. The crowds were blinded. But my visor let me see the horror of Icarus 2 as it was rendered into oblivion. The fiery carcass fell into the millions below before the explosion's shock wave hit us and knocked many to the ground.

Then the rest of Icarus 2 exploded on impact.

There was another blinding flash, and a plume of ash erupted from the cataclysm. The nearby crowds panicked even before they had picked themselves up—in droves, they surged from the tiered viewing platforms, swelling over the stairwells and gangways, and toppling from the tiered edges. Thousands must have been trampled to death.

I was struck back to my senses by the sound of my name as the wall of ash from the Icarus 2 reached us like a tidal wave and engulfed the area.

"Jaysid!" Odyssey 2 began to lift from behind me and rise into the dense ash cloud. "Captain!" A soldier smacked my helmet. "What the hell are we going to do?!"

My suit injected battle chemicals into my system, and now I had razor-like focus. "Keep comms clear!" I barked coolly. "Threat tracker's off, and the smog from Icarus and Odyssey is obscuring lines of sight. Switch to thermal charge detection and scan the platforms for guided missile systems. If O2 is gonna get hit, we're gonna hit first."

"What about the crowds, Captain? They're killing each other!" my sergeant radioed, her voice rattling.

"Nothing we do will stop that, but if O2 goes down, then everyone within the crash radius will die. Get to work!"

I motioned for my fire team to follow me. We were a three-man squad patrolling this section of the tiered chrome viewing platforms. We rushed to the first tier of the western platform—our silver reflective plating must have made us look like hellish, vindictive beings in the smog. The tier rose to shoulder height. A small spurt from our calf jets propelled us up, and we clambered awkwardly over the ledge and spread out into a covering formation. The people had surged away from the front and were crowding the access ways. Limp bodies lined the edges where they had toppled from the higher tiers or were scattered, trampled, throughout the platform.

"Can't see shit without the threat tracker, sir," the man on my right said.

"We've trained not to rely on that soldier, come on!" the man on my left said.

My thermal detector whined to life, and a green filter lined my visor. I began to pick up shapes in the smog. Five tones sounded, indicating objects which were highlighted in bright red displays at various points around the launch bay.

"Five possible launchers detected, sir, no idea on insurgent presence," the sergeant said over the comms.

"How the hell did they get those in?!" my lieutenant radioed.

"Threat tracker was laggy amidst the data noise, and crowds wouldn't tell a rocket platform from some space colony device," I answered. "O2 is rising, and thermal display indicates we have three minutes 'til weapons discharge. All fire teams, converge on the nearest launcher and neutralise it—along with all contacts."

Thirty indicator tag lights beeped on my display.

I turned to my fire team. "We're going to tier four up there, weapons hot."

We unslung our weapons, short-barrelled S-19 anti-personnel plasma arms. They were capable of firing high velocity, magnetic-induced plasma with enough heat to burn through any armour and enough power to negate any disrupting shields without superior amperage, like our own.

I powered on my weapon, and the blue indicator lights blinked as it whirred to life and rumbled softly with live oscillators. Whoever was attacking us was about to have a really bad day.

As one, we sprinted across the open platform and boosted over the crushing crowds, clanking onto the next chrome tier. This platform was practically deserted; we raced across and boosted to tier three.

A pale blue luminescent ball streaked past my head from tier four, burning a bright trail in the smog screen. It whisked past my shoulder with a faint crackling and impacted the chrome floor on the platform below with a sizzling ring.

"Contact!" I yelled and fired blindly at the ledge above.

My gun vibrated as the oscillators quickened to generate and propel my own plasma bolt. It streaked through the air like a shooting comet, passing return volleys along the way.

"Move up!" I ordered.

We advanced in a line, laying down a barrage of precise shots into the fog of war where the enemy fire had originated.

A plasma bolt hit my shoulder—the force of it made me stumble, but my disruptor shield ricocheted it up into the sky. The soldier on my right caught one directly to the chest and was flung back with a grunt over the platform edge. I heard the clattering and a wet groan as his winded body hit the ground, but I could not turn back to help him. My reading indicated only two minutes until missile launch.

I renewed my assault and rejoined the line with my remaining soldier in a staggered fashion as my comms blared with the battle chatter of other squads engaging the enemy. The High Command network also chimed within my helmet as other platoons engaged threats around the large area under the ascending bulk of O2.

"Blind them!" I ordered as the reader ticked down to one minute until missile launch.

I continued to advance steadily, laying down cover fire as my soldier wordlessly bolted forward while slinging his weapon. More plasma streaked down around him, but they hit wide of their mark. Visibility must have been even lower for them than us. *No battle visors*, I thought to myself. That meant the flash-bang would not be hindered from blinding them.

My soldier reached the far end of tier three, pressed up against the wall, and pulled a small device from his belt. He clicked it, and it began to whir and strobe. He lobbed it over the lip of the upper platform.

Forty-five seconds.

I sprinted forward as the ash and exhaust above were ignited with a blinding white light. I heard cries of pain and confusion and saw five writhing silhouettes in the fog above.

I initiated my boosters and fired at two of the clearest figures midair before the light died.

I clambered onto the ledge and fired at the vague areas of the other targets in quick succession. I heard only one death cry.

Thirty seconds.

I surged on towards the red highlighted image of the charging weapon—a tall obelisk alone on the platform. A plasma bolt knocked me off-kilter from the side, and I saw the dim shape of a scrawny assailant in the smog. I fired and killed him instantly.

A beam of red light pierced the gloom and reflected off of my silver armour plating in a dazzling array of colours.

"A laser?" These insurgents were archaic, but my armour was still reminiscent of the needs of the shelter gang wars.

I blasted the last assailant and approached the looming weapons platform. It was a tall cylinder twice my height, forged from dark steel like a shadow against the red highlight of my heads-up display. There was a missile perched on top, and it tracked O2 slowly as it rose from the ground.

Ten seconds.

I fired at the centre of the obelisk, hoping to melt it off balance and maybe fry the circuits. Another insurgent popped out from behind it to hinder me but was downed by my remaining soldier as he ascended to the tier. He joined me in firing on the missile launcher.

Five seconds.

The smell of ozone filled the dust-choked air, and the obelisk bubbled and sizzled from its midsection. The counter stopped at two seconds.

"Check on our man," I ordered. The soldier rushed back to the edge of the platform and leaped down. I heard his booster slow his descent as I frantically sent out a broad wave call, "Report! Will any missiles fire?"

"Charlie squad here, weapon neutralised."

"Echo, threat destroyed."

"Delta, all good."

"Tango . . . no tangos." That was Claudin.

I hated Claudin.

But the thermal scans showed no more red silhouettes. Battle still sounded in a dying chorus across the tiers, but the missile launchers were destroyed.

Odyssey 2 would ascend to The Space Cannon safely.

"Well done, soldiers."

# PART 3



History was now a mind-numbing fact of life to me, but when I was younger, it felt like the world was ending. If only I could fathom how true that was as a child—if only I could understand that even if the world was ending, more still could be ripped from me.

It was nearing the end of the twenty-second century when it started. Humanity had successfully moved away from unsustainable resources as a means of power and production. Parts of the planet, damaged by our meddling, had slowly begun to heal; we had a positive future in store for all life on Earth.

But then the sun failed us. Solar flares erupted with such potency that pinpoints of laser-like radiation would break through Earth's magnetosphere and destroy all below. Europe was stricken with the largest forest fires ever conceived, fleets of Pacific fishing vessels simply sunk into the oceans, and the ice caps melted 16%.

That was from the first three radiation falls.

Tens of millions died, fried in their skin, burned, or boiled, and many millions more had to be relocated, creating more strain on the reeling population of Earth. And humanity, without knowing a cause or cure for their plight, had to face its next challenge. They called it Solar Rain.

"That's the most ridiculous thing I've ever heard!" Dad cried in mock rage. "At least call it something cooler than *'Earth 2'!* What are we, morons?" He wiped spittle from his brown lips.

Our skimmer car coasted down the ocean road. It was a light, elevated vehicle with a glass dome that let us protrude upwards from the chassis itself. The height let us enjoy the blue aurora that spanned the skies. The aurora was a worldly phenomenon since the Solar Rain began, as the entire Earth's magnetosphere struggled to block the sun's constant, potent rays. It shifted colours frequently. There was some theory as to how the colour was loosely related to how close the next Rain would be, but it was not an exact science.

The road crested a cliff that jutted out over the open sea, tracing a narrow line between the gloomy inland forest and the sheer drop to the ocean. The waves crashed against the jagged cliff walls, gilded and glistening by the dimming light of the afternoon sun even as storm clouds moved in from the east to choke out the rest of the day.

"Honey, be reasonable," Mum smirked as she counted off on her delicate dark fingers. "There are . . . six different languages naming the star system alone. We need a simple name, for now, so Earth 2 it is."

"I reckon it's a waste not to call it New Terra. Now *that* is a cool name!"

"Really cool, Dad!" my brother said from the back seat. He was seven and found the idea of moving to a new planet exciting.

I did not.

"That's right, little Lathan! Just like your dad!" he chuckled.

Mum giggled too, but did not encourage him any further. "Just think how great it'll be, though," she said. "By the time you two have grown into handsome young men, the rail accelerator will be finished, and we'll be shooting off across the stars!" She shot her hand across the dashboard. "It'll take hundreds of years to get there, but it'll only feel like a few weeks for us. And by the time we arrive, the ship that departed minutes before us would have had decades to build our new homes!"

This was too much for me, and I finally let my anxious ruminations come tumbling out.

"But Mum!" I screamed, tears running down my face, "what if there's a mistake—what if we get on different ships? I'll be old before you get there, or you'll be long dead before I do!" The tears flowed freely down my face, and wet mucus ran from my sniffling nose. I was one of *those* nine-year-olds. "I'll be all alone!"

"Oh, my sweet Jaysid!" She rotated her chair to look directly at me, took my face in her hands, and gently wiped my tears with a comforting smile.

"Don't you ever worry," she said. "No matter what happens, you won't be alone." The aurora which silhouetted her flared bright red for a moment, then subtly shifted from blue to green. "You'll never be alone."

Both of my parents died three months later.

They were the lead scientists testing the radiation shields over emergency shelters, which were erected to protect people from the Solar Rain.

Like with many first endeavours, something went wrong.

Lathan and I were left to fend for ourselves. I protected him from the other kids in the orphanages, overflowing as they were with traumatised children—and from the adults too, when necessary. By taking on that responsibility,

I gave him the peace of mind he needed to follow in Mum and Dad's footsteps; he became a research and development prodigy, a talent desperately needed for the colony effort.

And I found out what I was good at while growing up: I was a protector.

# PART 4

## MARCH 2222—THIRTY YEARS LATER

"I still can't wrap my head around it, Lathan! The Wave One ships only hit the space cannon five minutes apart, but there'll be ninety years difference between them when they arrive?"

My dark brow was furrowed in concentration. I was sitting on a cramped, plastic armchair within our cramped living room. My wife Yasu sat on my lap and nuzzled my shoulder pleasantly, her silky black hair messing over her pale features.

"Correct!" Lathan exclaimed. "And it's only the thousandth time you've said those exact words."

"It's hard to wrap your head around," I said testily.

"Time is hard to do anything with, except to yield to," Yasu said gently.

"That's awful poetic of you," I nudged her playfully, and she poked her tongue up at me in response.

"Focus!" Lathan snapped. "You've almost got this figured out. I can see it in your stupid face!"

"Hey! My face isn't . . . ."

"Calm down, Jaysid," Yasu said. "He's only trying to help."

Grumbling, I piped down as Lathan eyed me with playful glee, expecting my retort. When none came, he continued as if nothing had happened.

"And by the time Wave Two rolls around, when the ships are built, and the Space Cannon has absorbed enough solar radiation to launch a few more times, one thousand years would have passed for the last ship of Wave One. Hopefully, Wave Two will arrive to a thriving terra-formed colony that wouldn't be too xenophobic about their distant, ancestral cousins showing up."

I stared blankly. "It still just does my head in whenever I try to think about it. Are you saying that when the last wave leaves, it'll be arriving at a five-thousand-year-old colony?"

"Four," Yasu corrected. "Four thousand years old."

My puzzled look prompted her to explain.

"Because," she said, "there will only be four gaps, between one and two, two and three, three and four, and four and five—four one-thousand-year gaps."

"God damn it!" I yelled. "My head is starting to hurt."

Lathan laughed heartily, removing his bulky glasses to wipe the tears from his eyes. "You haven't even begun to think about the more complex issues here."

"There are more complex issues?" I whined.

Lathan nodded giddily.

"The time frames don't add up!" Yasu said proudly.

"Correct! Five-minute intervals equating to ninety-year gaps with a six-month interval equating to one thousand years . . . it simply doesn't make sense."

"But," I said, "the new head of R&D, AKA the biggest nerd on the planet . . . no offence . . . has some magic, mind-hurting science thing to negate that, I'm guessing."

"Mhm," he nodded smugly. "And at the rate, we are going with this *science thing,* the intervals could shrink by half each wave. That includes the ninety-year intervals between each ship within a wave."

"Okay, I'll bite," I said. "How?"

"That is top secret, dear brother."

"Figures . . . all of these concepts just make me feel stupid."

"Oh, Jaysid!" Yasu leaned up and kissed my neck, sending tingles down my spine. "You're a genius in your own way."

"Thanks, hon," I kissed her forehead.

Lathan leaned back with a sigh. "Now, why can't I find someone like that to comfort me?" He sipped from his sweetened beer.

"'Cause you keep drinking that crappy sugar booze!" I kicked at his pudgy belly.

"Don't be horrible, Jaysid!" Yasu snapped, sitting up and glaring at me. Her expression softened as she turned to Lathan. "You'll find someone beautiful who appreciates your mind just as I appreciate Jaysid's, I promise."

"Yeah? We'll see," he grumbled.

I snapped my fingers. "What about that Cassiette girl from the mag-drive department? She's cute, and she couldn't stop awkwardly chattering to you at that social we all went to. You know, the one where I talked you up to that high-ranking science guy to actually get your name in the running for the head of R&D."

"You mean Claria from electro-mag propulsion?" He thought for a moment. "Nah, she's not into me!"

"Oh My God, you're thick for a genius!" Yasu said. "She was practically FAWNING over you in a cute nerdy way, and you were so oblivious it hurt me, but in a cute nerdy way too. She was gorgeous! You'd be perfect together—ask her out!"

"I don't know . . ." Lathan mumbled, raising his drink to his lips. Then he looked down at his belly and lowered his drink self-consciously.

"No hope for the colony if the smart eggs don't start making omelettes!" I jested.

"Hopefully, Wave One will have that all figured out before even Wave Two arrives. By the time we show up in

Wave Five, it'll be like living in a technological paradise!" Lathan said.

"I don't know," I thought aloud. "Look at the fanatics nowadays. We're used to death tolls by now, but two million by human hands? Not even by the Solar Rain? Hopefully, there will even be a colony and not a dead planet."

Yasu nuzzled my neck.

"Don't worry, Jaysid," Lathan said. "Remember what Mum said. No matter what happens, we'll be together."

The wall illuminated, startling us from our thoughts.

"An emergency broadcast?" Yasu said, "I hope another shipyard hasn't been lost to a Solar Rain. Those things are a bitch to repair!"

A grim-faced man appeared on the wall.

"This is an urgent communication. Due to recent insurgencies targeting key personnel and installations of the Colony Initiative, certain safeguards are being put into place.

"All scientific and research personnel class six and above are required to ship out on the next Wave; their intellectual and scientific knowledge can't be gambled on Wave One thriving until the next Waves arrive. In this spirit, we cannot gamble away the Colony effort under threat from fanatics. Therefore, personnel vital to construction and security of the colony effort must remain, despite any personal obstacles this mandate creates.

"For any enquiries please contact your relevant placement supervisors and roster officers. This is the end of the announcement."

The wall faded back to a blank beige facade again, and the three of us were stunned silent.

Lathan and I locked eyes. He was class nine in R&D, and I was the best security officer around; we'd soon be separated across the indomitable gulf of time and space.

"This is bullshit!"

I slammed my fist onto the desk's cool ceramic surface and immediately regretted it as my hand went numb. But I kept face, seething at the man sitting behind the desk with all the guile I could muster.

He was a scrawny, balding, necktie in a brown, drab suit, but he remained un-phased by my outburst.

"Take a seat, Captain," he said with disinterest.

"Jaysid," Lathan said gently from the desk chair next to me, "losing your temper is no use here."

"Ah, the cool head of a scientist. It's a shame your brother doesn't share that trait."

I was halfway down when I started again, but Lathan's calm reply halted me.

"Then you are misinformed, Mr Dell. Jaysid's cool head has saved countless lives, most recently at the Wave One launch. You may recall this event, yes?"

I settled down, quite amused with myself. I may have tried to physically intimidate probably the most powerful civilian in the region, but Lathan had successfully told him to watch his mouth. Mr Dell's disinterest broke for only a split second before he resumed with his dull monotone.

"No," he said, "I had not forgotten. My apologies . . . Captain." I did not reply. "But the fact remains, resource management and all, the fanatics have started targeting key personnel. It would be ludicrous not to send your brother to the new world ASAP. Humanity would waste him here. No meaningful improvements can be made to our colony technology with the time frames we're working with, and it would be a gamble not to send him to the new colony immediately in case Wave One failed."

"And what of our humanity?" I asked. "You can't separate us. Send me and my wife in Wave Two on his ship!"

"And those remaining would waste you, Captain. If I send you away, I'd be sending away one of our most capable leaders under fire. It was your suggestion to ditch the threat tracker that saved The Odyssey 2. Bogged down with all of those data points, we would have been ineffective in halting further attack."

"You can't be so naive as to think that the new world won't need security, law enforcement, combatants?"

"And you can't be so selfish as to abandon millions when they need you here!"

"Selfish?" I spat. "I have lost and sacrificed so much doing what I do for humanity—friends, my education, and the lives of my soldiers!"

"And humanity needs far more from you now, Captain, than it ever has. I'm sorry, but your request is denied."

"What of my R&D work?" Lathan asked quietly. "You'd be stopping us from reducing the time between Waves to less than a thousand years. The time gap would remain constant."

"That, Dr Moors, is simply a necessary inconvenience. The difference between a few hundred years and a thousand will matter little to the new Waves. No matter what argument you put forward, Doctor, you and your brother will be separated from each other. I'm sorry."

Lathan spoke slowly. "No, not separated from each other . . . you're killing us from each other."

Mr Dell sighed. "And the day is still young. I have thousands of requests like yours to process. Only a dozen will have enough merit to be considered, again . . . I'm sorry."

I looked to my brother, trying to take in his appearance as if it was the last time I'd see him. I observed his coarse black hair slicked back against his dark scalp, his thick-rimmed black glasses dominating his face, magnifying his brown eyes into huge bulges, and his lame, knitted jumper fitting tightly to his pudgy belly.

Only I could hardly see him from the tears in my eyes. When Lathan said the words, even though they did not make sense, they still hit me like a hammer blow. Once he hit the Space Cannon, he would be flung to the far side of space and time—he would live out his life on a world without me. When I arrived, he would have been dead for thousands of years already.

*No, not separated from each other—killed from each other.*

# PART 5

## AUGUST 2222

I stood within the swarming terminal of Wave Two, Ship Three, The Stella Drift. The names had improved somewhat. The terminal was a white-tiled expanse under a high chrome dome. Windows lined the top half of the wall, lending sight to the imposing ship beyond.

All around me, people shuffled along zigzagged cordoned paths, carrying the last of their possessions, checking them in to be loaded aboard, and saying their final goodbyes.

I stood before Lathan; Yasu was at my arm. I couldn't have done it without her beside me.

"I guess," Lathan mumbled, looking down at his feet as he shuffled from side to side, hands in his pockets, "I guess this is it."

A burning feeling welled up in my chest. My breath caught. "I can't do this . . . ."

"Shh," Yasu cooed, "it's alright."

I stepped forward. "Lathan." He kept his eyes down. "Lathan," I repeated. I touched his face and lifted it to look at me. Tears ran down from behind his glasses.

"Ever since Mum and Dad died . . ." he choked, "you've been there to look after me. I don't know what I'll do without you."

"Shut up, idiot," I chided feebly and then embraced him. "You have that scientist girl going with you now. Claria ain't no fool." I looked from our embrace over his shoulder to see her standing there. She looked on, standing by Lathan's bags and trying not to cry herself. "You'll look after each other," I continued. "You'll have nothing to worry about. A nerd like you—they'll make sure you have everything you need."

He coughed a laugh. "And you don't need to worry."

"I'm not."

"Liar," he smiled. "I know your biggest fear. Finding yourself alone in this universe. Even if I'm gone, you'll still have Yasu . . . like Mum said, you won't be alone."

My breath caught again, and I sobbed openly. "Travel safe, brother."

"Take care."

We parted, and Yasu rushed in to hug Lathan. "Don't let that girl break your heart, Lathan. I'll miss you!"

They kissed cheeks. "Look after Jaysid for me, Yasu."

"Oh, I will, don't you worry. He'll never be rid of me." She smiled, stepped back, and took my arm.

"This is it, I guess," he repeated.

We embraced one last time, and then he turned and strode over to Claria. I turned and walked away quickly with Yasu, tears streaking down my face.

"Jaysid!" he called out.

I spun.

"I'll tell my children to tell theirs, and to tell theirs, to look out for you when you arrive!"

I nearly broke down then and there—I would have if it were not for Yasu's presence.

I smiled through my tears and called back: "That's if you can actually manage to bed this woman!"

Yasu hit my arm. The people milling around stopped and gaped at my comment.

Lathan laughed loudly and held his middle finger up to me. I returned the gesture warmly. I then watched as he and his new love turned and passed through the gate.

"Goodbye," I said.

Yasu placed her head on my shoulder, stroking my arm. "You won't be alone," she whispered, "I promise."

One hour later, I was in my battle armour with my platoon, waiting on the perimeter of the launch bay. The crowds weren't allowed anywhere near the colony vessels. The threat tracker had been deactivated as per my instructions, and my unit was on high alert by the north partition.

The sky was veiled grey, and only a tendril of the blue aurora filtered through here and there—no Solar Rain in this region today.

The Stella Drift rose slowly atop a plume of ashen exhaust. It defied its weight, defied physics itself, to float daintily through the air towards the Space Cannon. A crushing feeling weighed heavily on my shoulders, but I shook it off; this was where Lathan was most vulnerable. I had to be alert.

The crowds raged. Some surged over the partitions and began to break through, heading for the tiered observation platforms. I switched on my plasma gun. It whirred to life, and the indicator lights blinked blue.

The unit followed my lead, and the breakaways stopped dead in their tracks.

The masses behind were still surging. I boosted into the air, soaring clear of the heads of the crowd, and I fired a plasma bolt across the top of them. The thousands gasped and ducked as it tore through the air and impacted on a building in the distance.

I fell back to earth heavily, collapsing onto one knee with a clatter. I stood slowly and eyed the masses.

Silence . . . .

"That was a bit much, sir, don't you think?" Claudin asked over the comms.

I didn't answer.

A different tone sounded: Command.

"This is Captain Moors," I answered.

"Captain, outer perimeter guards have successfully stopped infiltration. The launch is safe."

"How wonderful," I said dully.

Switching off my comms, I watched The Stella Drift. The roar of its engines from so far away sounded like a gently burning fire. The bulk breached the cloud ceiling and was lost from sight. Minutes later, a streak of light strobed across the cloudy veil.

The Stella Drift had been fired from The Space Cannon. Lathan had left forever.

"Goodbye."

# PART 6

## APRIL 2206—SIXTEEN YEARS EARLIER

The all-clear siren blared, and I looked up from the grey wall across from me. I was off shift, and I had nowhere to go. I had just the rumblings of my mind to keep me company—along with the rumblings of my empty stomach.

I was below ground when the Rain hit. So I just sat here in the alleyway sewer as the thousands—like-minded people like me who did not trust the shields to hold—all piled in the cracks and crevices beneath the city. We were like roaches hiding from the light.

Despite the throng, I was alone down here. Lathan had opted to trust his handiwork on the shield technology.

I hated my life.

But the sewers were clearing as people made their way topside to a radiated and blistered concrete hellhole.

"Hey there."

A pretty Japanese construction tech was smiling down at me.

"Hello . . ." I said back.

"You're a security soldier, yeah?"

"Yes, off duty, so I can't deal with any situations right now." I was too hungry to be bothered.

"Of course. Not why I came over though. I could hear your tummy rumbling from my hidey-hole down there." She gestured a nod down the narrow corridor. "Don't they feed you sec, guys? I thought that would be a priority."

"I gave my rations to my brother just before the Rain hit. He opted for a shield building despite my urging not to."

"Don't trust them shields, huh?" She slumped against the wall opposite me.

I didn't mind the company; she was easy on the eyes and seemed warm-hearted. But if I were to indulge in this conversation only for her to leave a short time later, I'd feel the loneliness more. It was better to keep to yourself.

She groaned and rolled her head as she massaged her neck. Locks of black hair fell from her cap and stroked her soot smudged face—such a lovely face. I guessed she could stay, for a bit. "My parents died in a shield early on . . . he says the shields are better now since his department has been working on them."

"Oh," she looked down. "I'm sorry."

"We've all lost someone," I replied. "He knows I hate it when he leaves me alone, though."

"Being lonely is tough. Believe me, I know," she sighed. "He sounds like he's in R&D. They don't feed them enough, so you had to give him your rations?"

"Some thugs . . . desperate kids, really . . . they jumped him this morning, stole his rations. I didn't need mine . . . I'm off duty. Nothing to use the calories for."

"That's lovely of you," she said.

"I look after my family. It's what I do. I protect people." I gestured weakly to the security badge on my jacket.

"Well," she said, "I'm off duty too." She pulled a ration pack from her pocket. "I usually only eat half at a time anyway . . . want to share?"

I let myself smile. "I'd hate to take from you."

She smiled back. "You're not taking—I'm giving. I hate being alone too, you know." She tore open the ration pack, snapped a dry bar in half, and tossed a piece to me. "My name is Yasu."

"My name is Jaysid."

"Jaysid," she smiled. "Don't worry, I won't let you be alone."

# PART 7



shuffled along ruined semi-urban streets. Chrome and quartz-laced structures with black dome ceilings rose sporadically into the bronzing aurora.

The colour made me nervous.

The cities were quiet now. One billion people had left the planet for New Terra on the last four and ever-growing colony waves. Since I was a boy, Earth's population had dwindled under the Solar Rains to the paltry ten million it was today.

But the difference was not lost just to the Rains or to the exodus of mankind, but also to conflict, crime, famine, scattering resources . . . and of course to fanaticism. And now it was worse than ever. Of the ten million left, five would leave with the last wave next month. Two million would remain behind, opting to stay and die with the world, or find new hope underground.

The other three million, statistically speaking, were likely to be dead by then.

Of those who would be left behind, perhaps a few thousand were of the fanatics, wishing to make sure no more humans escaped the fate of the Earth and affronted God. These fanatics believed that God decreed we had no place among the stars and must be snuffed out.

Their ranks were drawn from the children born into a dying world—young people already disenfranchised from a planetary womb that denied their protection from the cosmos. They knew nothing but pain, and of nothing but their impending doom at the end of a long road of violence and starvation. Without a guarantee for salvation on a modern ark to escape the burning floods, they wanted us all to stay, to walk into the holy light. That was the rhetoric they were fed, and it was easy enough to believe after the life they had lived.

They had claimed two more colony ships since Wave One, three whole shipyards, and immeasurable other lives and resources. We had pushed back; the fighting had been bitter, but it was our survival versus their death wish.

Survival had proved the stronger impulse.

I walked now towards their supposed last remaining stronghold. My feet trudged through the clutter, filth, and refuse that littered the area. Maintenance works weren't a priority anymore. My footfalls echoed past the mostly empty buildings.

I passed a ransacked facade here, an apparent bum there—quite a few bums actually, all milling towards a large warehouse down the road. We were disguised as vagrants to avoid suspicion as we converged from points all over the city.

"That's the building," Command chirped in our earpieces.

I rolled my eyes. "Get your hands off your ears, you incompetents!" Three of the milling hobos pulled their hands down from their ears with a start.

Command continued.

"Numerous shipments have been made to this warehouse—nothing declared openly. Without the support of any global authorities, the fanatics have been using increasingly less advanced weapons, and it's done a job of subverting our defensive capabilities. We think these shipments are something new . . . well, old.

"Luckily, the rail guns they used last time weren't maintained too well, or we would have lost two ships last Wave instead of one.

"Expect a mixture of these weapons when we breach—rail guns, plasma weapons, and laser beams, as well as sonic and static dischargers. Remember, you won't have full battle gear in there; you have small refractor plates under your get-ups that will diffract most las-shots—but for the sake of your disguises, your shield generators are now much smaller than you're used to. They won't stop a direct plasma hit, but hopefully, they won't have many plasma guns left. The oscillator fields with these smaller shields should thwart most rail gun projectiles, though, so watch for ricochets.

"Any questions?"

"Why don't we breach with an airship? Or better yet, blow it up from the sky? Why go in at all?" a man by me asked discreetly.

I didn't have my HUD without my helmet, but I could recognise the mischievous voice of Claudin.

There was an audible sigh from some sec soldiers now gathering on the corners out of sight of the warehouse.

"Because, soldier," Command replied sternly, "these could be innocents, this is a raid first, and only an assault should we encounter the fanatics. A breach from the air won't work because the ceiling is shielded from Solar Rain and nearly indestructible. The building's weakest points are the north end roller door and another on the south where it's too open for an assault, which is why it's being covered by snipers. We are going to punch through the north end with the rocket ram. If you do find them in there, drive them out into the open on the south side opposite from your entry point, and the snipers will take care of them. They have been instructed to treat any combatants on that side of the building as hostile . . . so don't break cover.

"Are you all good to proceed?"

"What numbers are we expecting inside, sir?" another asked.

Command paused before replying.

"Two dozen at the minimum, but likely many, many more. Remember, soldiers, we've raided and whittled down their fighters. This is possibly their last stronghold. Out of their thousands of supporters, they have maybe two hundred combatants left in this part of the continent. Don't be surprised to find them all in there."

The line buzzed with white noise as he kept the channel open for more questions. When none came, he grunted in a satisfied manner.

"Very well, green light to engage!"

I wish I could remember the assault. I know what happened, of course. I know we launched the rocket ram from the adjacent alley and crumpled the loading bay doors. I know we stormed the hazy breach en masse and encountered a warehouse teeming with surprised fanatics. I know we fought bitterly in a close-packed laser and plasma brawl that moved room to room, door to door, and hallway to hallway. I know that we lost more than half of our soldiers.

I could tell you all of that. But all I actually remember is a blurry, angry din.

My wits rejoined me as we cornered the last remaining fanatics in a large loading bay on the building's south side.

This bay was much larger than the one we had entered the building through, and the fanatics had time to reinforce themselves as we were bogged down fighting corridor to corridor. I was covered in blood, I could smell seared flesh, and I tasted vomit in my mouth. The air was thick with smoke, yet we fought on.

"Pin them down!" I ordered as my soldiers stormed the outskirts of the room and the gantries up above.

The enemy had taken a position by the open roller door. Crates and cargo had been moved outside as they attempted to flee, but our surrounding snipers pushed them back in. They took cover behind a makeshift battlement made up of their last metal crates.

This was it—it was almost done.

A plasma bolt streaked across the room and hit my shoulder. My meagre shield barely deflected it, but the force knocked me onto my back. A medic crouched over me, and his temple was seared open by a stray laser beam.

Cooked brains splattered over my winded form, and the medic slumped lifeless on top of me.

"They're dug in too tight!" my sergeant bellowed, her grim face covered with ash.

"If we duke it out here, there'll be no winners!" Claudin replied.

"We have to force them to break cover!" I barked as I freed myself from the corpse.

"How, Captain? They have a slow projectile tower in there which is repelling our grenades, and it'll take a grenade to make them break out under sniper fire!" my lieutenant said; he had moved up behind me with blood smeared over his face.

The citywide siren struck us from our discussion.

"Shit!" someone yelled.

The roller door on the fanatic flank began to rattle shut.

"They're about to feel even more boxed in! Prepare for a shit fight, boys!" Claudin yelled.

Someone yelled back, "We're all dead either way at this rate!"

"No!" I cut them off. "Disable that roller mechanism!" I ordered, pointing to the corrugated chrome roller as it rotated.

"Are you crazy, Captain?" Claudin blustered.

"Do it!" I barked. My tone stopped any rebuke short.

My sergeant and two soldiers from another unit opened fire on the roller mechanism with plasma bolts while the rest of us fought on. The metallic surface sizzled and sputtered but drove on downwards stubbornly. The fanatics yelled obscenities as they realised what we were doing, and their fire intensified towards the three shooters.

My sergeant went down with a wet grunt. The door rattled on.

The siren intensified, the high pitch wailing pierced deeper into the mind, blotting out even the din of battle.

"Suppressing fire!" I screamed—my voice raw.

The exchange of laser beams and plasma bolts was prolific. Like a billion refracting lights and haywire fireflies, the carnage engulfed the empty air. Both sides knew that this was the final push. They knew what an open door would mean.

The door creaked to a halt one-third of the way closed, allowing enough room for a whole vehicle to fit through. A second siren wailed from within the building.

"Warning! Warning! Radioactive shield compromised!"

"Warning! Warning! Solar Rain imminent, vacate the area!"

"Take cover!" I ordered.

The soldiers above retreated from the room. An orange hue descended on the world outside, and the ground blistered and sizzled.

On the ground level, we retreated as far as we could and took cover behind what was available. Several fanatics broke cover as the bright orange light shone through the opening, and they cried out as the moisture in the air boiled and sputtered. We gunned down all who broke cover, and the rest cowered, waiting for the end.

The full Solar Rain hit.

The light was like the flash of a nuclear bomb—bright, blinding, even behind cover, even behind my shielding arms and shut eyes. The paint on the walls blistered, and the crates melted or burst into flame. The holed-up fanatics screamed in agony.

The siren died out, and I clutched at the small concrete partition between me and the light. I could hear the heat, I could hear the sound of it in the air, in the materials around me, and I screamed.

I remembered my parents, and the pain they must have endured as they boiled in their skin. I remembered my brother and I, as children, all alone. I remembered him leaving through the terminal gate, and the streak of light his ship burned across the sky.

And I screamed all the harder, alone in this hell.

Then I remembered Yasu.

And I persevered.

The pain was unbearable. I thought of her—I thought of what I was fighting for. I had to protect the only family I had left and safeguard her life.

I focused on her face in my mind: the smell of her dark hair, her smile, and the way she chided me when I fussed over unimportant things.

The heat eventually eased off my gripping knuckles; an eternity later, the white light faded to a dull bronze and then dissipated entirely. The Rain had passed.

The safe siren blared, and I slowly crept out of my small cover, my armour cracked and partially melted. I was steaming like a demon straight out of hell.

"Casualties?" I asked over the radio.

"Prolific," came a garbled reply.

"From the Rain?"

"From the assault itself."

I nodded to myself solemnly.

My few remaining able-bodied soldiers closed in warily on the fanatic's smouldering last bastion. There was Claudin and a few others I did not recognise from other units. My lieutenant remained behind cover, dazed with shock. Everything was so quiet after the cacophony of the enclosed slaughter—after the terror of the Solar Rain. There was only the hissing of steam, the grunting of wounded men throughout the building, the sputtering of small fires, and the crunch of charcoal underfoot.

The area was a blackened mess. The defences the fanatics had used did absolutely nothing to protect them from the direct force of the ultraviolet radiation. Their blackened, charred bodies remained petrified in the position of their deaths. It reminded me of the eerie images of Medusa's victims or the city of Pompeii before it was lost to us again.

"We've got a live one!" a soldier yelled from across the room.

I frowned. "How?"

"Crawled to the far side of the room before he was completely cooked . . . won't last long."

I motioned some soldiers to the all but destroyed crates within and without the loading bay. "Find out what they were transporting," I ordered.

From among them, Claudin nodded sternly, all showboating gone.

I trudged through the debris towards the downed fanatic, ten metres further inwards. He found a small curb to cower behind and was now propped up against it, his back towards the loading bay doors. A soldier and a medic stood over him.

"Medical?" I asked.

The medic shook his head. "Wouldn't do him any good."

I looked down at the charred body that gasped and wheezed.

"Pain relief?" I asked.

"Wouldn't do me any good."

I glared at the medic and held out my hand. Begrudgingly, he handed me a syringe. I crouched down next to the dying man.

"Can you hear me?" The charred body stirred at my voice. If he still had eyes, he could not open them. If he could still talk, I would be surprised. But I persisted anyway. "Are there any more of you?" The body shifted, wheezing heavily. "What were you transporting?" I continued. Another shift, more wheezing. "Is your holy war over?"

The body coughed and wheezed some more. I realised he was laughing. I sighed and jammed the syringe into his leg. He stopped moving shortly afterwards.

"Twenty-three dead, forty-two wounded, many of whom won't make it."

I stood slouched in the aftermath as the other officers gave their report to Command, who stood stiffly in the coals.

"Did our snipers make cover?" another captain asked.

"All snipers got clear except for one pair. They stayed behind too long to keep the fanatics pinned," Command replied.

I winced. "Is it over?"

"We hope so, but we won't be celebrating just yet. Do we know what they were transporting?"

I shook my head, "It's all slag now, sir, molten steel."

He nodded thoughtfully. "Intel guesses they were even more primitive weapons to further undermine our technological defensive capabilities. What that could be, we don't really know. One crate is missing; it's unaccounted for on the manifest, it holds an estimated ten units. Even if it does subvert our defences, they wouldn't have the numbers to make any difference. It seems redundant now, but we'll be fitting each soldier with the best equipment we have against the last hundred years of warfare, just in case."

"Then it is over?" I asked. "They can't win even if they attack again."

"So it seems."

"And what were the global casualties from the Solar Rain, sir?" a lieutenant enquired.

The Commander sighed. "Two hundred thousand at an early guess. Shipyard Charlie caught it on the nose, one ship's shields failed in dry dock, and there was quite a high toll on our builders, too. The Rain came so suddenly many couldn't make it to cover."

I snapped from my battle-weary revelry. "Yasu!"

I rushed out of the broken roller door.

"Yasu! Yasu!"

I barged through our apartment door to find her making dinner—such a mundane thing.

"Jaysid!" she exclaimed with a start. "Are you okay? You look like hell!"

I nearly collapsed in the hallway, sobbing. "They said shipyard Charlie was hit . . . they said . . . ."

"Shh, shh." She rushed to embrace me. "I tried to call, but the interference was too intense. My shift ended right before the Rain hit, and I was underground in transit. Didn't even know it had happened until I arrived at the station." She laughed uneasily. Then her smile faded. "You really do look like hell." She jostled my mucky hair and stroked my grimy face, which was streaked with sweat and tears.

"We took the fanatic's last stronghold."

She gasped.

"We lost half of our assault force, and I think I killed more people than I ever had before." I shook violently as I spoke, feeling ill. She held my face in her hands. "But it's over, Yasu—they're done, we're safe. I wouldn't have survived if I didn't have you to hold on to. I nearly gave in, in the end there, but I held you close. Then I heard your shipyard was destroyed." I sobbed uncontrollably.

"Shh," she hushed again, "you're safe, I'm safe, I'm here, and you don't have to fight anymore." She caressed my neck. "We're together now." She held me close and didn't let go. "We have each other."

We made love that night under the blue aurora.

The soft spreading of blue light against the dark of night shimmered and cascaded over the sky like liquid silk, and our embrace tightened around one another, all that we had left in this dying world. I had fought to protect all I cared about for all of my life, my parents, my brother, now only Yasu. I lost them, but not her.

She sighed against my chest and ran her fingers up the nape of my neck.

It was the same for her. Since Japan had sunk into the sea, she had worked to build and safeguard all that she had left. Her little sister died from malnutrition when she was only young, her parents from skin cancers, and she was left with just me and Lathan. Now she had only me.

I looked into her deep brown eyes . . . .

We were two specks of chaff, adrift in this cruel cosmos.

She looked into mine . . . .

But we were not alone.

# PART 8

## FEBRUARY 2224

The fanatics had been silent.

With their militant arm gone, the true believers relinquished their crusade and acquiesced, leaving the launch port cities in peace. The others who elected to remain saw it fit to assist us. The spirit was cooperative yet remorseful. For all we knew, both decisions would lead to death—either from starvation, burning in the fires of the Solar Rain, or from suffocation in the cold vacuum of space.

But we shared hope, too, that each would find salvation.

For them, it would be beneath the earth, for us, above the heavens.

There were no onlookers by "Penny," our nickname for the penultimate ship. We called the last ship to leave

"Ult," short for the Ultimate ship in the Colony Effort. The names had gone down a peg or two again. Ult was moored twenty kilometres south of Penny. The only people around Penny were the crews, loading staff, and the rearguard security detail, my detail.

We were more relaxed than previous Waves. But that was no hard thing. The other ships in this last Wave had launched safely, and the first was moments away from being jettisoned from the Space Cannon.

My platoon milled around the semi-constructed area by a relatively small loading rampart off Penny's rear starboard side. I trudged with boredom as a dozen dock workers hefted the last of the cargo up the rampart into the white interior of the leviathan colony ship. The ground was lined with grey soil, built up over the months of construction, loading, and exposure to the solar elements with minimum maintenance.

The workers were pottering around the last crates, discussing what to leave behind for the stayers. They had delivered a last gift of fresh harvest for our journey, and the captain of Penny wanted to leave an equal portion of imperishable food in return, as well as half of our grain seed. We had more than enough for our own meagre colony crew with the acres of farm space we had on the ship.

"We should just leave the dehydrated stuff for 'em! It's not like they'll have the industry to make their own for much longer."

"Don't be so morbid . . . the condiments are more fitting—some easily processed goodness for them to smother their natural feeds in."

The chatter passed back and forth mindlessly as they worked. My eyes went from the grey dirt to Yasu sitting on one of the crates. She happily dug into a tin of peaches as her feet dangled just off of the ground. I didn't approve of her presence, especially not with a bronzing green aurora overhead. But she had felt uncomfortable on the ship while I was outside it.

Who was I to argue? Besides, we would be well on our way before the Rain hit.

"You've been going through those the past few weeks!" I kicked grey dust at her playfully, and she poked her peach-coloured tongue at me.

"It's not like I haven't been working my butt off building AN ENTIRE COLONY SHIP!" she snapped and then winked at me with a smile. "You're right though, not long after the fanatics moved out . . . it's all I can think of. I crave peaches!" She licked her spoon and upended the tin over her face. Juice and flecks of peach rained into her open mouth.

With a satisfied burp, she hopped off the crate and tossed the tin aside.

"Movement, Captain," the comms buzzed. "Delivery truck moving towards rear rampart."

I cocked my head and turned as a truck pulled easily around the corner of a building and drove towards us. I sensed my soldiers readying to fight, but the threat tracker, useful without the noise of millions of data points, detected nothing. No electromagnetic pulses, no plasma signatures, and no explosive tech.

"You guys expecting another truck?" I asked the workers.

One of the workers shrugged. "Didn't expect the first one."

I motioned Yasu to the porthole door by the rampart. She scowled but sensed my uneasy manner and slowly made her way to the door. I wordlessly ordered Claudin to guard her with my neural interface. He peeled off and tailed her casually.

Everything seemed to be fine, but my instincts were screaming. My mind turned to the missing fanatic crate. Ten units . . . but ten units of what?

I strode up to the vehicle as it pulled up. I felt confident with my laser refractor plates and a full disruptor shield. My soldiers all around the vehicle and on surrounding rooftops, along with the smiling delivery driver, reassured me even more.

He hopped down—a scrawny young kid dressed in greasy grey overalls—and closed the cabin door. He held a clipboard in both hands.

"Morning to you," he beamed. "Almost ready to be off?"

"Morning back to you," I replied. "That depends on what you've bought with you."

His smile was infectious. He was young, barely a man, and he seemed genuine. I could not help but return the smile even though I was wearing a face-concealing helmet.

"I have bought tools to help you step into God's light." In an instant, his smile twisted into a snarl, and he dropped the clipboard, pointing a crude object towards me, one too primitive for the threat tracker to detect.

"A firearm?" I thought aloud, astounded.

He pulled the trigger and the shot fired.

My disruptor shield was designed to deflect objects propelled by electromagnetism and was useless against a projectile without a magnetic charge—the bullet flew into my armour unhindered.

My refractive plates were designed to deflect lasers, not hard objects—they shattered, and the bullet passed through to reach the lower dermal layer.

The lower layer was designed to subvert shock weapons like a faraday cage and disperse sonic waves harmlessly, not to stop a solid projectile.

The bullet pierced these last layers and tore through my shoulder, knocking me down. The truck opened at the back, and the dozen fanatics cramped within poured out, carrying archaic gunpowder-based assault rifles.

"Slug throwers—take cover!" Claudin yelled.

Anarchy reigned free as the playing field was finally levelled.

The air filled with the sounds of plasma discharge, the sizzling of laser impacts into flesh, and the ancient, unfamiliar sound of gunshots.

I rolled onto my belly and tried to crawl for cover as blood leaked from my shattered battle suit. My heads-up display flared red, indicating severe trauma.

I could still crawl, though, I was not bleeding out yet, and I was still conscious.

"Yasu!" I groaned.

A gentler tone issued from my display, and it faded from pulsing red to a calmer rusty hue as my suit injected battle chemicals to counteract the gunshot. These drugs were a luxury we did not have when assaulting the fanatic stronghold.

The bleeding slowed, and the pain faded quickly as I dragged myself onto all fours, heading for the cargo crates. I was vaguely aware of the cargo rampart retracting, and of the raging battle.

More chemicals fed into my system, my vision cleared, and my groggy state shifted into hyper-focus. The blood ceased pouring from my wound.

I sprang to my feet and dove behind the crates as they splintered with bullet impacts. I unslung my plasma gun and switched it on. As it whirred to life, I looked at

Yasu being dragged into the porthole door by Claudin; it closed at the same time as the loading rampart.

Good—now I could focus.

I jumped from cover and fired. My blue plasma bolt hit one of the two fanatics charging towards me. It ignited the gunpowder in his magazine, and it exploded in his hands, incapacitating him permanently.

The second fanatic was the young man who had shot me. He had been trading fire with other soldiers while he charged my position, and he was drawn to me by his comrade's death.

As I aimed for him, I took in the whole battle. Several minor fire fights had broken out and spread in varying directions. Despite their weapons levelling the playing field, the fanatics were outnumbered, and none had made it to the ship before being gunned down.

The fanatic had his sights on me first and pulled the trigger. I flinched back, but nothing happened. He had run out of bullets. I smiled—no wonder we had moved on from these weapons.

I sighted to fire, but then the Solar Rain siren sounded.

I immediately brought up a map on my heads-up display. All my men were within running distance of safe shelter, be it the ship or the surrounding buildings.

"Disengage!" I ordered. "Seek cover and keep them outside!"

I broke cover and sprinted for the porthole door at the base of the ship. I saw other soldiers heading to various other doors and shielded structures while trading potshots with the few remaining fanatics.

All fanatics heading for cover were gunned down or pinned in the open—all save for one.

I was maybe ten metres from Yasu's door as the atmosphere started to bronze. I could see her there, egging me on from the porthole window on the door. I smiled between strides.

I was going to make it.

I was tackled from behind into the brightening grey dust, and my gun clattered away beyond reach. Sprawled in the dirt, I looked up to see Yasu's horrified face in the window. The heat of the air intensified as the wailing siren blared. I pushed myself up from the ground, but the fanatic elbowed me in the kidneys with the full weight of his body.

Even with my armour and battle stimulants, it hurt. I was winded and face down in the dirt. My enemy straddled my body and pummelled the soft areas of my armour at the back of my neck and at my sides.

Struggling to dislodge my attacker, I noticed my comms going wild as the air sizzled and brightened to a searing bronze.

"Captain! Deploy the mag parasol, or you'll fry!"

"It's never been used in the field, he's done for!" Claudin said.

I tuned them out as I rotated and knocked my assailant savagely in the face.

The threat tracker pinged on my heads-up display. "Warning, distance to safe shelter insurmountable, deploy magnetic parasol. Be advised: 87% chance of failure, resulting in traumatic death."

That was comforting.

I struggled to my knees and drew a tent peg-like device from my webbing. I took one last look at Yasu—almost too bright to see—I smelled the blood on my shattered plating burning. The bronze light reflected off the silver plates and turned me into a burning beacon.

"Solar Rain imminent," the tracker chimed.

I rammed the peg into the ground, and it expanded three metres into the air.

"Deploying magnetic parasol."

The tip of the pole flared and whirred, creating a shimmering dome three metres wide in diameter.

"Solar Rain descending."

The shimmering dome exploded in all the colours of the rainbow, cascading down the surface in waves towards the ground as the magnetic shield atop the parasol refracted the ultraviolet radiation away from me.

"Deflection unsustainable, 98% integrity and dropping."

"Shit," I muttered.

I was tackled again. The young fanatic was within my rainbow dome. I shuffled with the momentum and stayed on my feet. We squared up against each other as he pulled out a large knife. My armour was not immune to such primitive things as that, either. He lunged and slashed rapidly, and I retreated under his onslaught.

"75% integrity."

He slashed at my shoulder, and I sidestepped as his blade swiped through empty air and the tip passed through the rainbow wall. He withdrew his blade and noticed he now only had three-quarters of a knife—the tip was a red-hot smouldering stump. I dragged my gauntlet across the colourful cascade and grimaced as my knuckles burned, but then I brought my red-hot fist into the stunned fanatic's face before he could recover.

He screamed in agony as I seared and ripped burned flesh from his face, and he stumbled back, dropping the knife.

"50% integrity."

I pressed the advantage. He fought back hard, but only managed to injure his fists on my armour. He moved in to grapple with me and tried to push me against the wavering wall.

"40% integrity."

We struggled there for a while. He was just a malnourished kid. I was a trained soldier, well fed and equipped, but wounded. The balance tipped back and forth between us.

"30% . . . 20%, warning, integrity failing rapidly."

He swung at me, and I ducked under his attack. His hand passed through the threshold into hell, and he screamed in agony again, pulling a charred and smoking black hand back into safety. I struck him in the ribs—a sickening crack punctuated the roaring from outside, and I pushed his head towards the wall. He resisted fiercely, but centimetre by centimetre, I pushed him closer. Then his hair went through the wall, his toes slid across the threshold, and his knee.

He screamed.

I didn't care.

"10% integrity."

He screamed harder as I kicked his knee to buckle him down and I pressed half of his face against the threshold.

"5% integrity, prepare for magnetic parasol failure and imminent death . . . Solar Rain lifting."

The parasol broke, and we were both struck by the intense heat and bronze-tinged atmosphere. My armour crackled and blistered, and the fanatic collapsed into the searing ash and molten glass. But the light was returning to normal, and the temperature was quickly cooling to survivable levels.

I left the fanatic there and sprinted for Penny's door, my feet kicking up flecks of molten glass as I ran.

My comms buzzed: "He's alive?"

"What a beast!" Claudin roared.

I reached the door to see Yasu's distraught face. I pushed the open button . . . nothing. She was frantically trying to open it on her side, too. I switched to the ship's channel to find a heated debate raging.

"Can't leave them out there, they have families on board!"

"And open us up to more fanatics? No, my responsibility is to those aboard this ship—those outside can get to Ult before she takes off."

"This is Captain Jaysid Moors," I cut in, "I am trapped outside with roughly a dozen soldiers, please unseal the doors." My voice was cracking, and Penny's engines were starting to rumble.

"I'm sorry, Captain, I have seven hundred thousand people to think about on this ship . . . goodbye."

"No!" I screamed. "You can't separate us! We're so close!" I was yelling into a dead line; they had cut me off.

I threw my helmet off and slammed my fist against the glass, calling Yasu's name. I could see her screaming mine as she frantically tried to pry open the door, but our words were cut off from each other. We couldn't even say goodbye.

My men rushed from the surrounding buildings in similar states of bewildered panic, rushing towards the ship's doors as the engines spewed forth fire and exhaust. I slammed my fist against the glass again and heard a crack. It wasn't the glass. I slammed my broken fist again and again with such force that my gauntlet shattered and crumbled from my bleeding hand.

The ship rumbled uncontrollably and lifted from me. Thick exhaust filled the air, choking me, while Yasu's face became too obscured to see.

"I love you," I saw her lips say before she was almost completely hidden from sight.

A soldier grabbed me by the neck, pulling me back from the rising monolith. "We have to leave, Captain! We have five minutes before Ult lifts off—they won't wait for us!" he screamed.

The exhaust engulfed us and pushed us around in torrents, but I didn't budge.

"He's jacked up on battle stims! Someone help me!"

Four other soldiers dragged me towards the personnel carrier by the ship as Penny floated unnaturally into the air, out of reach.

"Yasu . . . I love you!" I sobbed.

I was alone.

We stumbled over a body, the wounded fanatic who robbed me of my family. Somehow I had found his broken knife in the debris and put it to his throat, seething down at his ruined body.

"I hope you're happy!" I spat.

My soldiers rose around me, watching as the personnel carrier started and roared towards us, its floodlights cutting weakly through the exhaust of the ship. I moved to pull the knife across the fanatic's throat, just a young, crippled kid . . . I thought of Yasu.

How she chastised me when I lost my temper.

The sound of her saying my name as she ran her fingers up the back of my neck.

The way her hair fell messily across her face when she danced.

The way she poked her tongue at me.

I looked down at this burned boy, at his stubborn hate, his hideous wounds compared to Yasu's soft features and gentle nature. This zealot's only family was perhaps the bereft youths now dead around him, or the manipulative leaders who radicalised him. At least I had known a family—he had known nothing but pain, seeking to cause it in others, and had succeeded. And yet, with Yasu's memory firmly in my mind, all I felt was pity for him. I dropped the knife in the dirt.

"Captain, we have to leave!"

I looked to the personnel carrier. Two soldiers guarded the open rampart at the back, and one waved me on desperately. I looked back down to the fanatic and released my grip on him as I stood.

"Survive. Live as long as you can in this dying world, and I hope one day you grow wise enough to realise the evil you did this day. Survive and repent."

I left him there. The carrier's doors groaned shut and cut us off from the tumultuous world outside. We were silent, contemplating our losses.

"How far will we be separated from them?" one asked.

"If we enter the Space Cannon five minutes after them, there will be a forty-five-year time difference between us. Once they slow down enough at the new world, we will still be travelling at relativistic speeds, and another forty-five years will pass between us before we arrive . . . ninety years." I spoke slowly, without any emotion, understanding the concept perfectly for the first time in my life.

"How do you know, Captain?" another asked.

"My brother explained it to me before he left on Wave Two eighteen months ago . . . three thousand years of time dilation between him and I when we arrive."

"Let's hope that the other Waves all survived the ages, otherwise we will have to build from scratch."

"Don't we already?" I asked.

The silence was overpowering.

Ult left one heavily guarded door open for us. We drove right on into the cargo bay, and she lifted off shortly afterwards.

Leaving the atmosphere was unremarkable, grey and smoggy; fire, smoke, and the like obscured our view of the land. As we entered space, we were treated to the sight of a greying blue-green world enshrouded by the ever-changing aurora. I'm sure I would have found it beautiful, if I were not watching Penny enter the tracks of the Space Cannon.

There was a streak of light jettisoning from the cannon, and Yasu was gone forever.

As we approached the Space Cannon base, a small transport left it and docked with us, ferrying the six hundred Cannon personnel to Ult and putting our numbers just shy over three hundred thousand. They had initiated the final acceleration procedure, and Ult drifted into the metallic half-pipe track that extended thousands of kilometres into the void.

There was a humming as the Cannon's magnetic acceleration affected our hull. I was watching Earth as we were fired. This little dot, this morsel of dirt, was supposed to be our home. The pulsating star that once gave life to it now bore down with relentless intensity, and we fled its wrath. This place was supposed to be the thing that bound us as we looked to the stars, together as a community, and now it was a hollowed-out husk, a battlefield of ash and broken families. The Earth became a streak of light, and we were flung into the cosmos as my own world shattered into a million pieces.

# PART 9

## JULY 6224—FOUR THOUSAND YEARS LATER

We spent three weeks sailing through the void at relativistic speeds. I expected to see the stars streaking past us like bright lines, forming a tunnel around our path. But in reality, we were only travelling across a few solar systems. The stars, for the most part, were light-years away and remained fairly stationary. Perhaps the closer ones shifted into red or blue wavelengths of light as we travelled towards or away from them, but to see a streak of light from a close-by celestial body was as rare and as fleeting as seeing a shooting star.

The reason our journey took weeks and not years was a bitter pill to swallow. It was the top-secret technology that Lathan had been working on, which we were now all privy to: The Graviton Engine. It was able to manipulate the gravity field we produced, essentially negating our mass and allowing us to break the light speed boundary without causing every single atom on board to explode.

The science had always escaped me. But I knew that if the scientists that left on Wave Two had stayed, the Engine would have improved exponentially, shortening the time dilation between Waves from millennia to centuries, and the time between ships from ninety years to a mere decade or even less.

If Lathan was not forced to leave me, the time between Yasu and I would still have allowed us to live a life together. As I said, it was a bitter pill to swallow.

The reassurance of a short journey and only being ninety years behind the last ship elevated the colonist's mood. But to me, it did not matter—a day's journey or a thousand years, my brother would still be dead when I arrived, and Yasu would be too.

I was alone.

The soldiers from my unit were suffering the same grief, but they were of little comfort. I was finished. New Terra would provide no salvation for me. Despite this, the more chipper of them tried to keep us unified, inviting us to the ship bar to nurse our drinks silently and keep an eye on one another. It was a nice sentiment, but the wounds were still too fresh.

The Graviton Engine slowed us down closer to our destination, causing us to merely travel at millions of kilometres per hour and leave relativistic speeds. We could see our new sun, stable and whole, and a tiny planet in the distance, bristling with satellite activity and the like.

The previous Waves had thrived.

A coasting journey that would have taken days was shortened to hours as the New Terrans accelerated our ship externally through some unknown technology. We docked at a mammoth space station orbiting one of the three moons around the blue-green planet. The planet was clear and pristine, lit warmly by golden light from this system's star, a benevolent sun providing warmth and energy freely without causing harm.

The station itself was a disc world hanging in the sky, open to the vacuum of space. Yet within the city on the surface of the disk, crowds of thousands were milling around freely, without space suits or any protection to speak of. The disc world must have supported its own atmosphere.

We touched down gently on a broad expanse which rimmed the city. The captain was understandably nervous to open the airlocks, but was eventually assured of our absolute safety and complied with station command.

My unit and I waited on board for hours as the hundreds of thousands of the last colonists disembarked. We made vague promises to each other that we would stay in touch and eventually disembarked lethargically as the ship cleared. The air was warm and clean, and the sky was as of night. New Terra obscured the entire horizon, covered with vibrant blue oceans and deep green continents like old Earth. The terraformers on Wave One had worked splendidly, and the cities could not be easily seen from space. We had kept our lessons from before the Solar Rains and preserved our new home well.

I bustled through the customs line, set up like on the tarmac of an airport, and was eventually greeted by a pale, slender man with no eyebrows in a featureless grey suit.

"Welcome to customs station, Earthling!" he said enthusiastically.

"You speak English?" I asked, surprised.

He sighed, probably sick of the question. "Yes, we practice all the classical languages for new arrivals to integrate smoothly. You're the last ship, though, so now I'm sure it'll just be taught as tradition."

"I see."

"Name?"

"Jaysid Moors."

"Travelling alone? Or are you expecting family to greet you here?"

"I'm alone."

He frowned at this "Hmph . . . it says here you have a greeting party waiting . . . must be a mistake, then. Carry on through."

"Huh?" I was cajoled through the gate before I could enquire further.

My hopes rose momentarily, but if it was Yasu, she would have to be over one hundred and twenty at least. It must have been a mistake, as they were literally processing hundreds of thousands of arrivals. My hopes faded bitterly.

I stood alone in the milling crowds as the new colonists—along with my unit—were diverted to stations to be allotted temporary lodgings and community or work placements for integration. I ambled towards a sign labelled 'security and defence' but stopped short.

An elderly woman stood smiling, clutching in one hand the arm of a shy seven-year-old. And in the other hand, she held up a holographic sign that read 'Jaysid Moors.'

I walked up to them through the crowds, uncertain. "Hello?" I said tentatively.

She looked at me knowingly, and her smile beamed with warmth.

"Jaysid?" she asked with a frail voice.

"Yes?"

She looked familiar, but there was no way she could be Yasu. I kept my guard up.

"I'd know you anywhere. My name is Aiko, Yasu was my mother . . . and, well . . ." she looked right at me, "you are my father." She stepped forward quickly and embraced me; it was gentle, firm, and loving, like a dear grandmother's hug.

"What?" I choked.

"Yasu carried me before she boarded Penny. She gave birth to me on Natera down below." She gestured towards New Terra. "And she told me of the sacrifice you made to keep her and I safe."

"Yasu was pregnant? It can't be . . ." I croaked.

"I know," she cooed and held tighter, "I know."

I broke down and fell to my knees. My smouldering grief finally surfaced and cascaded through my whole body. She held me even tighter, and I winced back as she squeezed my injured shoulder. She stood back, concerned.

"My bullet wound from the fanatics," I tried to explain through gasps of air. She took my broken hand in its cast. "From when I tried to break into Penny to get to her," I explained further. "Aiko . . . I'm so sorry, Aiko." She held my cheeks as I continued to ramble. "You came here to meet your father, and you found this blubbering mess . . . Yasu, she must have passed away . . ." I choked again, "by now."

"Jaysid . . . Dah," she corrected. "Mah told me the stories, how she screamed when you were shot, how she watched you battle that cruel man under the full brunt of the Solar Rain. She told me how it took several men to pull you from the ship as it rose away from you. For me, it's a tragic history, but for you . . . you've only just lost her. Dah, I can't imagine what that was like for you, and I couldn't be more proud to call you my father!"

I looked up into her dark eyes. She had to be at least ninety but she looked barely seventy. She was a gentle blend between my dark skin and Yasu's paler complexion. Her hair was greying but undoubtedly brunette, and her smile perked up at the corners of her mouth, reminding me of Dad and Lathan.

"Aiko, my parents died when I was young. I know what it's like. I wasn't there for you Aiko, you were alone—I put you through that! I'm so sorry."

"Hush now, Dah, don't be stupid. I had Mah, and we found distant offspring of your brother, Lathan. You'll like some of them," she chuckled. "Look at me! Being all grandmotherly to my Dah. Up you get. We'll head planetside to a good clinic I know and get those wounds mended proper. It'll take a weary five minutes but it's still pretty amazing technology these days—it took five hours to heal a broken bone when I was growing up!"

She continued to prattle pleasantly as we rose, and she guided me through the crowds.

"And don't you worry, Dah, we weren't alone. She was surrounded by friends and family when she went. We have some of them setting up a little welcoming party for you back home; she built up a whole community, and they all can't wait to meet you. We have so much to talk about! Oh, this is Sarna, by the way." She gestured to the little girl skipping along besides her. Sarna shrunk behind Aiko as she was introduced. "She's your great-granddaughter, but you won't get too much out of her today. She's quite shy. I'm minding her while Jussy—one of your grandchildren—is off on the outer rim of the system holding a mining summit or some such. Don't worry, she'll be back to meet you in an hour or so. You'll have plenty to do over the coming weeks, so much family to meet, and stories to tell. We are quite comfortable, but I'm sure a man like my father would have no trouble being snapped up by any self-respecting security firm should he wish it. You're probably one of a hundred people who've actually been in any long-lasting conflict to speak of. Punks around here still need a good smack on the bottom!" She sighed. "Punk is the right word, yes?" she asked. "Oh, and my husband's nephews all want to meet you—they'll be about your age so you won't be babysitting them, don't you worry," she laughed.

She prattled on as I took it all in, gobsmacked. Day trips across the solar system, minute healing technology . . . family formed by Yasu, even descendents of Lathan.

Everything I had ever known and loved was gone. Everyone I had cared for was dead. But here, my daughter chattered warmly while my great-granddaughter poked her tongue at me like Yasu used to do.

All my fears had been realised, and then laid to rest. I still had to work through the grief of my losses. But Mum was right: I was not alone in this universe. No matter what happened, I would never be alone.

# A NOTE FROM THE AUTHOR

Thanks for reading Solar Rain!

**Your review would make my day!** An honest review on Amazon or Goodreads helps other readers find this story, and keeps me writing books for amazing readers like you.

**Want more?**

Prepare yourself for a bonus short story:

## MINOTAUR STRIKE FORCE

# MINOTAUR STRIKE FORCE –
# A SCIENCE MYTH SHORT STORY

## PART 1 – UNEARTHED

His passing was muted in the confined stone tunnels; by moss, webs and dust accumulated over millennia. Compared to the muffled boot clack against stone, every other sound was terrifyingly loud.

His breath rasping in his throat.

His blood pounding in his ears.

The incessant, thundering beat as the monster pursued him.

He tried and tried again to get a signal on his wrist pad; tapping at it with sweating fingers, causing the screen to miss click and shift, but it was no use anyway.

But the labyrinth walls were too thick.

He turned a corner and sprinted into a dead-end, slamming into an ancient wall with a nose cracking thud.

With a grunt he fell back, sprawled against the ground as the dimness exploded in light and colour and pain. But he did not lose consciousness.

The ground still trembled beneath him with every footstep of the approaching creature. *Boom, boom, boom.*

No amount of dust and moss could dampen that sound.

"Come on, Ali," he spat blood from his mouth and forced himself to stand. "Follow the markers, think, think." Wiping the tears from his eyes, Ali turned around; searching the junction he had just rounded. Around an adjacent corridor, there was the pale purple glow of one of his expedition's markers.

For a fleeting moment, he let hope get the better of him.

But that hope was dashed as quickly as it had taken him, as a monstrous roar echoed throughout the labyrinth.

Ali dashed towards the light, around a bend, and down another darkened corridor. He wiped his hands on his jacket and spoke into his wrist pad as he ran, making a recording.

"Mayday, mayday, this is Ali Demirci from the Oxford archaeological expedition in Crete. We need help. We uncovered something in the ruins and it's killing everyone! Please send help to these coordinates." He finished the message and queued it to broadcast as soon as his wrist pad had a signal.

Dashing over exposed roots and crumbling pavers, ducking around tight pathways and following the illusive amethyst glow of the markers, Ali desperately tore through the maze. And all the while, the incessant boom of the beast that pursued him grew louder, faster.

Ali tripped over nothing, falling down an incline with a yelp, and landed on his face.

If his nose wasn't broken before, it was now. He tried to blink away the light that exploded in his vision. But it did not fade, instead, it persisted. He realised he wasn't seeing stars because of a potential concussion; he was seeing *moonlight*.

He gasped, wiping blood and tears from his face. The entrance to the labyrinth was ahead. The courtyard his team excavated glistened in the light of the full moon.

"I'm going to make it!"

There was a snort from up the incline, and Ali paled. He turned slowly, balking at the misted breath that puffed from the hulking shadow that loomed over him. It obscured the entire hallway, silhouetted by the eerie purple archaeological light.

"Oh my God!"

Fear overrode everything else; pain and exhaustion were nothing compared to the terror of the beast. It scraped its hoof against the ground, igniting a brief spark that lit up its damp fur, matted and slick with blood that dripped from gnarled horns. Its bloodshot, yellow eyes caught the brief spark of light and retained a crimson glow after it faded. The moonlight glinted off the bronze ring set into its nose, and off the glistening sweat and viscera.

Ali upped and bolted, and the Minotaur stampeded after him, rampaging down the incline and through the tunnel with a thundering fury.

A history major and archaeology dork, Ali was no athlete; but in his terror, his legs found new strength and his lungs found new air. The decaying walls and frescoes flashed past him in a blur as the mouth of the tunnel yearned for him.

He tripped on a root at the last step, crashing head over heels into the courtyard to sprawl in a coughing, spluttering mess.

He shifted onto his back, clambering away from the tunnel as the rampaging beast charged and he covered his eyes, waiting for the end.

But the thunder stopped. The beast snorted in derision.

Ali risked opening his eyes.

It had stopped on the threshold, staring him down from the dark with murderous intent.

Ali's wrist pad lit up—his message sent—and he cried out in relief. "Yes! YES!" Despite the pain in his limbs, he leaped up and jumped for joy. "YES! You can't leave your labyrinth while you're still protecting the artefact! Hah!" Ali fist bumped the air, spinning to halt dead in his tracks.

A line of dark figures watched him, the moonlight illuminating their military gear and weapons, their faces covered with dark helmets and balaclavas.

"Oh, that was fast, thank God you're here!" Ali hobbled forward, "My team, they were torn to pieces by that thing! I only just managed to get out." But he stopped before reaching them. The fear, the same fear that propelled him from the Minotaur, was now rising in his chest as he watched these soldiers. "You aren't here to help?" He said.

One soldier tilted his head. "We need to make it look like he was gored." He drew a knife, which shone wickedly in the moonlight.

"What?" Ali stepped back.

"He squeezed off a distress signal, Sergeant." Another one said, looking at his wrist pad.

"Well, we better hurry then." The sergeant said, and stepped towards Ali.

# PART 2 – THE RESCUE SQUAD

## KIERAN AHMAD

Kieran rolled and tucked away his prayer mat as the Hippogriff banked steadily through the night sky. The Moon was full, and the sky was clear, shining into the observation room where he went to pray—it was the only place the rest of the Griffins left him in peace.

Not that he minded their attention. They were his squad, after all, his family.

He slipped out of the observation room, the door sliding shut behind him as he stopped in his tracks.

"Sergeant!" Jason leaped back from Aideen as she pushed him away.

"What are you doing back here, Kieran?" Aideen said.

"What's this?" Kieran was a big man, tall with a barrel chest. He crossed his arms and looked from his corporal to his lance corporal, putting on his best, fiercest gaze.

"Don't be a dick, Kieran," Aideen said in her usual quick style, so quick that the words squeezed on top of one another as she spoke them. "You know damn well what's going on here and you have for weeks."

Kieran eyed her, she eyed him back; Jason nervously glanced between the two.

Kieran broke first, his stern visage breaking into a smile. Aideen broke a split second later.

"You two need to be more careful than that. I pray here."

"Yeah, yeah," Aideen waved him off.

"And Isao comes here sometimes, too." Kieran finished. "And you," he pointed at Jason. "You are a good Griffin. I inducted you into this team, took you under my wing. You're good but distractible. I know Aideen will keep her shit locked down on mission, but you need to know that if this interferes in any way with you doing your job, I *have* to report it to Ev, understand?"

"Yes Serge."

"Good, now wipe the lipstick off your face and get to the armoury. Ev will be briefing us soon."

Kieran walked past them as Jason touched his lips, and chortled to himself as Aideen slapped him.

"I'm not wearing lipstick, you ejit! Kieran's just shit stirring."

He made his way through the mess of the Hippogriff, where Bhanu was polishing her boots. "You trying to start a fire, Ev?" Kieran asked.

"Stow it, Sergeant." Bhanu said, "And you know I hate it when you call me Ev. If you must use my last name, can you say all of it? I don't call you, *Ah*, Ahmad. And do you know where Aideen and Jason are? I just pinged the squad to assemble. Isao and Solvi are already gearing up."

"Aideen and Jason tried to make fun of me for praying." Kieran said, as Aideen and Jason filed into the room behind him.

Bhanu finished polishing her boots and pulled them on, looking at Kieran with one dark brow raised, "Discrimination?"

"Hah!" Kieran slapped Bhanu on the back, "I give Aideen way more shit for her religion than she does mine! You're a funny one, Captain."

"Just get downstairs, Sergeant!" Bhanu snapped. But she smiled knowingly as Kieran turned away from her. "Griffins will be Griffins."

The briefing started two minutes later in the cargo hold and armoury of the Hippogriff.

"Griffins," Bhanu nodded at her squadron, "Lucas and Mon are dropping us into an archaeological dig in Crete. High command thinks they just triggered a booby trap, but seeing as the whole team has gone dark, they're sending us in, just in case."

"Why though?" Isao yawned. "I don't disarm traps. I hunt monsters."

Bhanu glared at Isao. "How's your hearing, Private?"

Isao straightened up. "It's getting there, Cap'n."

"It would be a damn sight better if you treated the last op as if it was a genuine paranormal threat *before* it messed you up."

"What do you think?" Kieran asked as Solvi elbowed Isao in the ribs.

"Best case scenario, it is just a booby trap . . ." Bhanu glanced at Isao before carrying on. "Worst case, based off the distress call audio, which I just sent to each of your HUDs, a guardian class entity."

"Will we be taking in specialist ammo for this one?" Jason asked, leaning forward.

Bhanu chuckled, "You want to take specialist ballistics into a ruin?"

"I . . ."

"Griffin High Command wants a standard recon load out until we can confirm paranormal activity. They don't want to explain to UG that they spent their budget annihilating a member country's heritage jumping at shadows . . ." she glanced at Isao, ". . . again."

Isao shrugged, "But I wasn't jumping at shadows, it was a . . ."

"Yeah, yeah," Jason interrupted. "I'm just concerned by the lack of equipment."

"Don't worry, Lance Corporal," Bhanu said, "My Hippogriff is always fitted with a vast array of ammunition. If the mission requires it, we call in an

OWAU situation, fall back, and then blow the ruins to kingdom come."

"All right!" Kieran bellowed, "Let's go jump at shadows!"

Bhanu shook her head, "Get ready to wrangle, Griffins. Talons down in five!"

The Hippogriff—an Aerospace Capable Armoured Personnel Carrier—swung into a holding pattern over the exposed courtyard.

This AC–APC was a peculiar model. It was large enough to take up most of the courtyard, with a bulky central fuselage, angular wings and tail, and a protruding cockpit that formed the shape of a beak. This was not a happenstance design; it was the signature vessel of the Griffins, a branch in Global Response that boasted the most capable soldiers known to the world.

Global Response – Fable Infringement Necessity: G.R. - F.I.N.

A harsh floodlight pierced the night, lighting up the dig site as it was buffeted by winds churned from the Hippogriff's propulsion jets.

"Those archaeologists were thorough." Lucas, the Hippogriff pilot, commented to his co-pilot, Mon.

"Not thorough enough," she said forlornly.

The dig site was a large sunken pit with four dirt walls and surrounded by excavated soil. A large subterranean level—an atrium or courtyard of sorts with ancient broken pavers—had been exposed to the world in the top of a cliff head overlooking the Aegean Sea, which shone dull grey under the moonlight. There was an unoccupied campsite by the dig site, which had a grand view of the water beyond the cliffs. The clustered spires of the coastal cities shone like beacons on the horizons, their light pollution blotting out most of the stars, passing satellites, and space stations.

The rear rampart of the hovering ship lowered and the squadron waiting within were buffeted by the torrents. They were not overly perturbed by this, as they wore full combat armour. This included black and bronze fatigues with the Griffin insignia on their shoulders, sophisticated armoured plating and heavy-duty webbing holding an assortment of high-grade military weapons. Their armour was completed by full, face concealing helmets. The face plates locked down in place to resemble a griffin's beak with orange visors depicting hawkish eyes.

"One body sighted," Aideen pointed to a sprawled form in the centre of the courtyard, lit up by the Hippogriff's search light.

"Roger," Bhanu nodded, reading from her wrist pad, "Lucas, Mon, it looks like we might not have clear comms within the structure. We're going to set up line-of-sight signal relays as we sweep the ruins. Keep a holding pattern over the courtyard and be prepared to turn it into a kill box."

"Aye, Captain!" Lucas chirped over the comms.

"Good hunting, friends." Mon said after him.

"Sergeant," Bhanu said to Kieran, "Your fire team takes point."

"Sure thing." Kieran started barking orders, "Aideen, Jason, we're dropping in and securing the landing zone. Captain's moving in after us. Do *not* keep her waiting."

"Yes, sir!" Jason attached a line above the loading ramp to his armoured vest and dropped down, zipping groundward as he spun slowly, sweeping the courtyard with his high-powered assault rifle.

Aideen was a split second behind him, then Kieran. The three touched down within heart beats of each other and quickly swept the area.

"Clear," Jason said.

"Clear," Aideen parroted.

"Bhanu, the floor is yours." Kieran said over the comms.

As Bhanu and her fire team followed suit, zipping down with Isao and Solvi, Kieran's team focused their aim on the entrance to the ruins. Once the second fire team had touched down, the cables retracted. Then the Hippogriff broke away, gliding into a circling holding pattern over the courtyard.

As Bhanu's team moved up behind Kieran's, Aideen sidled up to Jason and spoke not over the comms. "Your dismount was a little slow there. Shame you were faster the other night."

"Oh, I think you were satisfied, eh?" Jason returned.

"Guys," Kieran said, "This is not the time or the place."

"Sorry, Sergeant," they both said in unison.

Kieran shook his head, "Don't turn me into an asshole by making me tell you to knock it off while we're in the field."

"Sorry, Sergeant," they both said again.

"You *are* an asshole, though," Aideen said, nudging him.

"That's beside the point," Kieran said, deadpan.

"What have we got?" Bhanu and Isao moved up on their flanks, covering the entrance while Solvi examined the body and set up a radio relay. It had two satellite dishes, one pointing into the sky to be picked up by the Hippogriff, and one pointing into the tunnel. She had several others strapped to her back.

"I don't like it, Cap'n," Jason said, his tone was now serious. "You said intel suggests a guardian type entity, but that poor sap behind us isn't *in the ruin*. If it is an entity, why did it pursue him past its limits?"

"Ruin is labyrinthine in nature," Aideen added. "Given the area . . . could this be . . ."

"A Minotaur." Kieran said.

"Solvi?" Bhanu said.

"Nothing on the body ma'am, ID matches the distress call. His wounds are odd though, a clean gore, which seems . . ."

"Odd," Kieran said, "This isn't a straight up op, Bhanu."

"Well," Bhanu was processing the situation at a million bits a minute. "Oxford says this team was looking for a fragment of an artefact in a suspected temple of Poseidon. The jewel of the Aegean is a fragment of some icon that is said to hold significance. If there is an entity present, it means the artefact may be more than academic."

"Ev," Kieran said, "That doesn't explain the neat gore wound."

"Should we drop specialist ordnance?" Jason asked.

"Our orders haven't changed." Bhanu said, "We don't call down ordnance until OWAU is confirmed, *especially* if we don't know what we're up against yet. We follow our orders, search and rescue, seek and destroy if needed, and recover any supernatural artefacts *if* they exist."

A low, drawn-out growl reverberated, echoing out of the tunnel entrance.

The team readied themselves, training their weapons on the dark opening.

"That was a distant echo." Solvi said.

"Then we close the distance," Bhanu said, "Griffins, move in."

The team moved into the labyrinth as the Hippogriff kept vigil from above.

# PART 3 – THE LABYRINTH

## BHANU EVERLY

The choking sensation of claustrophobia washed over Bhanu immediately as they moved into the main conduit leading into the ruins. It was made even worse by the half-collapsed frescos and caved in ceilings the further in they travelled. Then there were the gnarled mossy roots exploding out of the walls and floors.

The very atmosphere was entrapping.

The Griffins had state-of-the-art HUDs on their visors, which helped them to see in low light environments. But they still needed the lights fitted to their weapons so that they didn't smash into roots or other protrusions along the way.

They crept up an incline, moving in a leapfrog fashion, covering one another as they progressed. Eventually they came to a three-way fork marked with a fading purple glowing lamp post and a fresh red glow stick.

"Next lamp post spotted," Kieran gestured down the left corridor.

"Roger that," Bhanu said, "Solvi, radio relay."

"Yes, ma'am." The squadron covered Solvi while she placed another relay, pointing one dish back towards the entrance and the other towards the next marker light left by the archaeologists.

"There's another red glow stick by the next purple lamp post." Isao said.

"So, the archaeologists had backups?" Aideen suggested.

"This doesn't feel right, Captain." Kieran said.

"I agree." Bhanu replied.

Solvi finished setting up the relay. "Come in Hippogriff. Can you hear me?"

"Aye, Solvi, Aye we can." Lucas crackled over the comms.

"There is a lot of interference," Mon said. "I can track you on the radar, but I can't guarantee coherent comms the further you progress into the structure."

"Roger that," Solvi said. "Ma'am, we should progress as if we are on our own."

"Agreed. Griffins, follow the markers, we set up radio relays every other junction. And above all else, do not get separated."

"Motion detectors pinging, Captain." Jason was reading from his HUD, "But as far as I can tell, there's probably several tunnels and even floors between us and the entity . . ." he trailed off as the walls rumbled with earth quaking footsteps. Dust and gristle fell from the ceiling with every step.

"Oh, we've got a big boy," Kieran said. "This one is going to be a good one."

The squadron spent the next half an hour moving cautiously through the maze of ramparts and corridors and twists and turns. They followed the fading succession of lamp posts and freshly cracked glow sticks. They placed their own markers—fluorescent yellow glow sticks alongside the radio relays—as they went.

"I can't tell how far underground we've gone." Kieran said to Bhanu quietly.

She checked the compass on her wrist pad. Like the one overlaid on her HUD, it read '*NA*', "How's your sense of direction?" Bhanu said.

Kieran pulled a little brown cube device from his pocket, which had its own compass read out. It spun chaotically. "It leaves a lot to be desired." He said.

"You know we can hear you two whispering?" Jason mumbled.

"Am I going to hear you complaining?" Bhanu said.

Jason turned back to sweeping the tunnel ahead, the lights from the squadron failing to pierce the deep gloom.

"We may have needed a second team," Bhanu said.

"Nah," Kieran replied, "It's too tight and compact. All they could do is wait outside and come in after we don't report back, and then die themselves . . ." Kieran trailed off as the Griffins all turned to face him, their visors resembling glowing orange eyes in the dark. "I mean, *worst* case scenario."

"Bell end," Bhanu said, "Griffins, keep moving."

Around the next bend, Aideen held up her fist and went into a crouch. The Griffins shifted silently to the walls and obtrusions along the path.

"Light spotted," Aideen said.

"The archaeological lights?"

"Negative . . . well . . . yes, but there's some kind of blue shimmer down that way."

"Water?" Isao asked.

"If there was water, it would reflect the red and purple given the lighting, not blue." Solvi swatted the back of Isao's helmet.

"Ow."

"Griffins," Bhanu said, "Lock it down, and push forward."

They came into a wide chamber of deep blue stone tiles; it was a central node of sorts with other dark tunnels and offshoots funnelling into the one place. It was as big as the courtyard outside, and the roof—three metres high—glowed with phosphorescent light that bled through the bluestone in a flowing, tessellating pattern.

The walls and floors and patterns in this room were somehow unmarred by the passage of time. Within the centre of the chamber stood a dais with an altar carved from pure sapphire. Upon the altar was a dark golden prong with a sharp point. It looked like it has been snapped off at the bottom from some larger object.

There was also the ruined equipment of the archaeological set up, with scattered crates, broken work lights, and mangled bodies.

"Well, we found the rest of the archaeologists," Isao said as the team moved into the chamber, covering the different hallways branching off it with precision.

Some of the blood seeped into the phosphorous patterns, channelling into the depressions and glowing crimson.

"These bodies are much more bloodied up than the guy we found at the entrance." Jason noted, "The difference is night and day."

The Griffins cracked glow sticks and tossed them down each darkened hallway, illuminating them in yellow, showing pits, dead ends, and junctions.

"Looks like someone's been trying to remove this artefact from the dais too," Solvi said, kicking away a discarded blowtorch.

"Well yeah," Isao said, "The whole reason the team was here in the first place was to recover the artefact, no?"

"No," Kieran said.

"Yeah," Aideen chimed in, "This site is a wet dream for people like this. Taking a blowtorch to it would be like cutting the Mona Lisa out of her frame with a hacksaw."

"I didn't know you were a historical connoisseur," Kieran said, "But she's right, Bhanu, something here doesn't seem right."

"I agree," Bhanu said.

Kieran watched her. Even though her face was obscured, she knew that Kieran knew she was frowning.

"We all thinking the same thing?" Jason said. "Phantom ops?"

"Why do you immediately jump straight to the bogeyman?" Solvi said.

"Well, for starters, we're counter paranormal soldiers. Why is it always hush hush when those rumours about a clandestine paranormal agency come to light?"

"Probably," Bhanu said sternly, "For the same reason United Globe covers up our operations." There was a tremor and a roar from a hallway, and then the unmistakable sound of gunfire.

"An archaeologist?" Solvi suggested.

Bhanu sighed. The quaking booms grew closer, faster, the gunfire grew louder. "Archaeologists do not have automatic weapons." She checked her weapon and took aim down a tunnel. "Whoever killed that man outside has pissed off the entity and is leading it back this way. Prepare for combat, Griffins!"

# PART 4 – BULL MAN

## KIERAN AHMAD

Bhanu had picked a hallway seemingly at random. But, without question, the rest of the team took up a position around her. They aimed down the same dark recess. Bhanu may have been a stern leader, but she had damn fine instincts, and not one of her Griffins would question them.

The trailing dust from the ceiling came in larger torrents as the creature thundered closer. Kieran could feel his heart swelling up in his throat, but training kicked in and his hands remained steady.

There was another burst of gunfire, which lit up the tunnel around the corner. It was followed by a roar and a cry of pain. A soldier in black military fatigues flew around the bend and slammed into the wall with a crack.

Before he could fall from the wall, a hulking, shadowy figure charged into the dark recess and slammed into the soldier with a sickening squelch. The labyrinth trembled as dust fell from the ceiling around the slaughter like flowing water, illuminated dimly by the Griffin's lights.

With a snort, two jets of haze puffed away, and the figure tossed its head. The soldier's body was flung from its horns and it slid to a stop by the tunnel entrance with a thick trail of blood in its wake.

The creature snorted again and sighted the Griffins.

Yellow bloodshot eyes lit up red under their torch lights. It scraped its hoof against the ground and lowered its horns.

"Minotaur!" Jason squeezed his trigger and opened fire on the beast as it charged.

The corridors were narrow, and the beast was enormous. It barely squeezed through, even stooped low to charge. It tore out of the tunnel as six streams of fire tore into it. The bullets were useless, pinging off its thick hide and ricocheting off its horns as it barrelled into the room, knocking away crates and bodies both as the Griffins dived out of the way.

The path of the Minotaur continued until it smashed into the other side of the chamber. The Griffins, having scattered from its path, took aim and resumed fire.

"We need armour piercing rounds!" Isao barked as his gun ran dry.

Before he had finished speaking, he ejected his mag and slammed a fresh clip in place, continuing his stream of fire with only a split-second interruption.

"Hippogriff, come in!" Bhanu pinged Lucas and Mon, but all she got was static, "Shit." She quickly took in the situation as the Minotaur righted itself and lunged for Solvi with a hulking hand.

It grabbed her ankle and tossed her down a hallway as if he was a doll. She hit the ground hard and skidded, clambering for a hand-hold before she fell into the deep pit.

"Sod it, Griffins, back the way we came. Kieran, Jason, guard the artefact and get Solvi out of that hole. Watch for more unknown combatants."

"How do we get it to follow us?" Isao panted as he dashed past Bhanu and back the way they had come.

"I've got an idea!" Aideen dashed towards the beast and skidded under its swipe, unloading a whole clip from her sub-machine gun into its face.

The Minotaur roared and flinched back. Aideen took that opportunity to spring up and grab a hold of the thick nose ring protruding from its snout. She yanked it hard, her visor misting as the beast snorted in pain, and then leaped back before it could thrash its horns to gore her.

Aideen bolted for Bhanu, who turned and sprinted after her down the corridor. As she ran, Bhanu turned to fire on the beast to keep it engaged, and make it follow them.

"Kieran!" Solvi cried as she scrambled for purchase and slipped further into the pit.

"Stay on the artefact!" Kieran shouted to Jason as he dived down the tunnel; sliding on his belly over the moss to grab Solvi's hand. "Oh, shit." Kieran's eyes widened as he quickly realised why Solvi couldn't pull herself up.

The floor of the tunnel and walls of the pit were covered in slick moss, which squelched as they slid further down, pulling Kieran further over the side as he held onto Solvi's hands.

"Sergeant!" Jason cried after them.

But he was too late. Kieran and Solvi plummeted into the dark abyss.

# PART 5 – PHANTOM OPS

## KIERAN AHMAD

Kieran braced himself to plummet to his death.

In the last few seconds of his life, he imagined sharp rocks or spikes or a pool of acid waiting below.

Instead, the reality was *much* worse.

He and Solvi landed in a damp pile of discarded carcasses and refuse. Rats, squirrels, and rotting wood. They slammed into it with a sickening squelch and a rising stench that almost made him vomit inside his helmet.

Their helmets *were* vacuum capable, but they needed an air supply to make that work which wasn't needed for this operation. So, unfortunately, they were subjected to the stench of decay.

"I should have let you fall to your death," Kieran wheezed.

"Piss off," Solvi pushed him from her and clambered to stand. She was covered in gunk. "I should have pulled you under me as we fell."

"Kieran!" Jason shouted from the tunnel. "Solvi, you alive?"

"Unfortunately!" Kieran bellowed back, "We're going to try and find a way up. Guard the artefact and stay alert!"

"Sure thing!" Jason called back.

"You and me, Solvi," Kieran said, "We're going to navigate this place like rats in a maze. Smart rats, understand?"

"A maze with a very hungry cat and other stranger, meaner rats prowling the shadows?"

"Come on, Solvi. There ain't nothing meaner than me."

Kieran's flash light failed to pierce into the deep gloom as the sound of distant gunfire—accompanied by the tremors of the rampaging beast—reverberated dully throughout the walls.

## AIDEEN KELLY

Adrenaline thrummed through Aideen's veins and her pulse pounded in her throat as she sprinted through the ancient corridors with Isao and Bhanu in tow, taking turns to fire back at the charging beast.

She sped around, skidding through dust accumulated over centuries as she stopped and pivoted. Her panic rose as she waited for Bhanu and Isao to round the corner and dash past her, training her sights on the fluorescent lit corner of the ancient ruins.

First Isao came, then Bhanu, then the Minotaur.

It gouged deep marks into the stone with its hooves as it struggled to turn, igniting sparks which lit up its rippling, wet furred musculature. It snorted, two jets of misted breath shooting from its nostrils, and its bright red eyes homed in on Aideen.

Training overrode panic.

Griffins were sourced from the best soldiers in the world, warriors who faced the unknown and survived against all odds. Once selected, they were subjected to months of rigorous psychological training to complement their military knowledge, and taught how to fight monsters.

Without it, she was sure she would have buckled and ran.

Instead, Aideen exhaled and fired a short burst. Four bullets erupted out of the muzzle of her gun, strobing the walls in harsh yellow light. The Minotaur flinched back as the shots struck its hide and ricocheted into the surrounding walls.

"Enough fire, Aideen," Bhanu called back, "It's pissed, it'll follow us."

"Too bloody right," Aideen was already sprinting, letting her natural urges to flee have their way with her legs. She caught up to Bhanu and Isao in an instant.

"Are you able to raise the Hippogriff?" Bhanu shouted.

"I'm getting a stronger signal now!" Isao said.

"Why though? I thought we set up bloody relays!" Aideen said.

Isao was barking into his wrist pad as they sprinted down the corridors. "I have a faint connection! Lucas, Mon, come in, we have an OWAU situation, I repeat, OWAU, we need armour piercing rounds. Come in, Hippogriff!"

Lucas's garbled reply blared through as they tore past more radio relays and drew closer to the entrance. "I read you ground team, confirming OWAU, Our Weapons Are Useless, armour piercing rounds requested. Mon is readying a heavy weapons drop and the Hippogriff's talons are primed."

"Roger Hippogriff, danger close, we've got a Minotaur."

"Roger that Griffin, good luck!"

As they rushed past another relay, the connection went static again. Their device was shot to shit.

*Sabotage,* Aideen thought.

"Shit, Kieran, come in!" Bhanu yelled into her comms, but there was more static. "Shit!"

"Should be the next few bends," Aideen said. *I hope the others are all right . . .* She thought, dwelling on Jason and the last kiss they shared.

## JASON ARMSTRONG

Jason stood alone in the central chamber. The light had a shimmering quality to it, rippling as if disturbed by the Minotaur and the gunfire.

That would have struck him as odd, but he had been in many counter-paranormal situations before. This was par for the course.

What was putting him on edge, however, was the unknown combatant and the way the team was separated. Griffins worked together, always. If they were ever separated, it meant things had gone catastrophically wrong. And this op was a mess from the start.

He glanced at the body of the strange combatant.

The soldier was well equipped, almost as well equipped as Jason was. So he had to be on his guard. Those men were clearly here for the artefact. And they had clearly killed that archaeologist outside.

They would kill him if he was caught lacking.

It wasn't like he could take cover here, either. Every bit of cover opened him up to flanking fire from another corridor. He considered making a barricade out of the crates, but he suspected he did not have enough time before the enemy made themselves known.

There was a scrape in the distance, an echo of a footstep and a harsh *click-clack* sound. Without a moment's hesitation, Jason aimed down a corridor and opened fire.

The hallway was illuminated with the strobing flash of his weapon, and a dark figure ducked back behind the corner.

"Screw this." Jason grabbed a grenade from his belt and pulled the pin.

Before he could throw it, a shot pinged from another corridor. It clipped him across the shoulder. His armour deflected the bullet, but it staggered him mid-throw.

The grenade flew wide, bouncing off the wall and rolling across the chamber floor.

"Oh *screw* this!" he shouted.

He rolled behind the altar as more gun fire chipped the floor around him. The grenade exploded, the concussive boom blasting against the walls with fire and shrapnel.

The altar cracked—crystalline sapphire shards spraying the area—and the artefact tumbled loose from its perch on the as Jason was floored.

Coughing, bleary-eyed with ringing ears, Jason was struck momentarily by the sensation of a great wave crashing upon the shore, and then he was back in the chamber. He grabbed the cracked altar with a bloodied hand and pulled himself up.

*That's not good,* red smeared the cracked blue pedestal. He couldn't feel any pain.

*You're in shock . . . Was this from my own grenade? Those bastards . . . the artefact . . .*

A flash of blue and bronze in the dimness—crashing waves and roaring oceans in his ears—the artefact flashed out at Jason from the floor and he clumsily picked it up and slipped it into his webbing.

Several dark figures rushed in from the surrounding corridors.

Jason couldn't really see them. In the smoke and debris that choked the shimmering air, all he could make out were shapes. But despite his dazed state, he had good instincts, and his HUD showed him movement as a dotted representation at the bottom of his cracked visor.

He reacted with extreme prejudice.

He held his rifle in his good arm and fired a burst from the hip.

The first figure toppled, and the second figure fired back, a pinpoint of strobing light in the haze. Already crumbling, the dais crumbled into shards as the stream of fire missed Jason.

With a burst of return fire, the second figure slumped to the ground, silent.

Footsteps.

A figure blindsided him, rushing through the smoke from another corridor and tackling him over the dais with a grunt.

The rifle tumbled out of Jason's hands, but he was already drawing his pistol as he used his numb arm to keep the attacker at bay. Two shots into the abdomen knocked the black clad soldier from him, two more shots to his head made sure he wouldn't get up again.

The space around him erupted in bullet impacts again, and Jason dived for his rifle. As adrenaline did its work, Jason struggled through the pain, feeling was returning to his arm. It was a dull ache coupled with an intense burning sensation. Despite the pain, despite several of the bullets striking his armour plating and knocking him around, Jason grabbed his rifle in both hands and sighted a muzzle flash down a corridor.

These men were good, well equipped, tenacious even. But Jason was a Griffin. He had faced worse, and he wasn't going down without a fight.

And the artefact, it pulled at his awareness; it wanted to flow; it wanted to smite.

A shot smashed into his chest-plate. He held his ground without faltering and returned fire. His target cried out, and then a shot struck the back of his knee. His armour was lighter there, flexible. The bullet tore through Jason like wet paper.

Jason roared as he fell to one knee and pivoted, downing the soldier who had crippled him.

*Was the ground shaking?*

"I need support." He was shocked when blood splattered over the inside of his visor when he spoke. But he kept his nerve, kept firing, and keyed his comms. "Sergeant!"

## KIERAN AHMAD

Kieran stopped in his tracks with Solvi on his heels. The ceiling shook with a violent clamour, and chunks of debris fell onto them.

"That was a grenade!" Solvi cried, "Jason, Jason, come in. Skit," she swore in Swedish, "Still can't raise anyone."

"We're only one floor down from the radio relays," Kieran grimaced. "We should be able to at least get a garbled transmission."

"Well, the situation demands we improvise, Sergeant. That was a grenade, so we should start thinking out of the box." She fumbled around her webbing, pulling out a satchel which she leaped up and slapped onto the ceiling. It stuck with a wet plop.

"Are you seriously suggesting we detonate C4 inside this historical site?" Kieran's visor glinted in Solvi's torch light.

"It's been compromised by gunfire and grenade blasts, and our squad mate is in danger."

"I agree," Kieran was already taking cover around the next corner, "I just wanted to make sure you understood. Light it up!"

Solvi dashed around to join him and clicked a button on her wrist pad. With a powerful blast that rocked the Griffins, the C4 blasted the ceiling to smithereens. Debris and dust rained around them as the shock wave blew past the corner, dampened by their armour.

"Sergeant!" a garbled transmission broke through in a blast of static. It was Jason.

"Come in Jason," Kieran and Solvi were already sprinting through the dust cloud towards the rubble and clambering up through to the next floor, using the fresh hole they had just *excavated*.

"I'm taking heavy fire . . ." there was more garbling, not just static, but coughing. "Multiple shooters, I can't hold them!"

"You can and you will, Griffin, backup's almost there, just hold on!"

# PART 6 – DECIMATION



## LUCAS DEANS

There was an uptick in chop as Lucas swung the Hippogriff over the landing site.

"You drunk up there, pilot?" Mon's perpetually judgemental voice crackled in his flight helmet.

"I cannae deal with ya nonsense, lass! Prepare to drop the heavy artillery."

"Cargo drop is primed, *lad*. Just say the word."

"I'm gon ta swing around ta provide covering fire as soon as we drop. Harness yourself!" From the cargo ramp, Mon looked at the harness rack, and then gripped firmly onto one of the support rails. "Three, two, one, mark!"

The cargo ramp shot open. High winds surged into the cargo hold and Lucas fought to keep the Hippogriff over the landing zone until the indicator light beeped.

Mon's voice came over the radio, "Successful drop. Pivot!"

Lucas pulled hard on the stick and banked the Hippogriff to hover over the hastily dropped crates in the centre of the excavated atrium.

"Spinning the gun now!" Lucas said.

He held down a secondary trigger on the stick, and a whirring hum built up. The Gatling gun under the Hippogriff's nose spun to full speed.

An image popped up on his flight visor's overlay. It depicted the tunnel with a chaotically gyrating reticle. "Chop's keeping me off kilter."

"Then get *on* kilter!" Mon huffed as she clambered into the cockpit and threw herself into the co-pilot's chair.

"How did ya get up here so fast, ya crazy lass? Were you harnessed in?"

Mon was flinging straps over her shoulders and donning her own flight helmet, "But of course. I have the stick, focus on the gun."

"Roger." Lucas took his hands off the stick.

Now that Mon had the flight controls, she could focus on steadying the Hippogriff in the chop as Lucas focused on aiming the gun at the entrance. The reticle's chaotic gyrating on his HUD steadied. The winds were still an issue, but Mon was as good a pilot as Lucas. She kept the Hippogriff still enough.

"I see movement!"

"Friendlies?"

"I cannae tell . . . wait. Friendlies and enemy contact on top of one another!"

## AIDEEN KELLY

Aideen, Bhanu, and Isao sped down the tunnel as the Minotaur slammed into the last corner behind them.

"Light, I see the Hippogriff's light!" Isao cried.

"Ground team," Lucas's voice was much clearer over the radio now, "I have the entrance covered and the heavy weapons have been dropped. Clear the tunnel, now."

As they scrambled for their lives, the rumbling stampede of the monster threatened to overtake them.

Its misted breath condensed on their rear armour plating.

Its horns scraped the ceiling above them.

They sped out of the tunnel and dived onto the ground, spinning and bringing their weapons up to train on the Minotaur's head.

But the beast halted, skidding with scraping hooves by the lip of the tunnel. It glared with glowing red eyes as its horns and nose ring reflected glints of the Hippogriff's flood light.

"It stopped." Isao said.

"I don't have a shot yet!" Lucas barked over the comms. "Draw it out."

"It won't follow," Aideen realised. "It won't follow because it's a guardian. It's here solely to protect the artefact."

"So . . ." Isao sat up, his gun still trained on the Minotaur. "Now what?"

"Get your new weapons, Griffins," Bhanu was already on her feet. "Sooner or later, that thing is going to go prowling for the others. We need to be the ones hunting it by then."

———·····∞———····◯····———∞····———

## KIERAN AHMAD

Kieran sprinted into the central chamber with Solvi on his heels, their weapons sweeping back and forth. But all they found through the clearing smoke were bodies, a cracked, empty altar among the detritus of a vicious gun fight, and a downed Griffin sprawled over the dais.

"Jason!" Kieran sped to him, skidding to his knees to take him in his arms, "Jason, no."

His blood glowed crimson over the phosphorescent tracings. His chest was still moving with rapid, shallow breaths.

"No targets," Solvi swept the tunnels, "Over half a dozen dead hostiles, artefact's gone too."

"Sergeant, I . . . I couldn't hold them . . ." Jason's voice was a choked sob.

"Shut up, Jason. You did good." Kieran was searching his body for wounds.

Jason's armour was pilfered with bullet impacts. Several had gotten through and blood gushed from the holes. His right arm was a blasted mess of charred blood, and his helmet visor was cracked open.

Kieran could just make out one of Jason's eyes, listing between consciousness and oblivion.

His rifle was discarded to one side among a sea of shell casings, and his knife—dripping with crimson—was clutched feebly in one hand.

*He got hit with a grenade.* Kieran realised. *After the grenade did its work, the enemy would have swarmed him. But he made a damned good account of himself.*

"Jason, I'm so sorry."

"Took the artefact right from me . . . couldn't . . . tell Aideen I . . . I'm sorry." He gasped, his body shuddered, and his biometrics flat lined on Kieran's HUD.

"Sergeant," Solvi spoke with a sternness that wavered. Her emotions were bubbling up inside her. "Sergeant, we need to go after them, we . . ."

Kieran couldn't quite hear what she was saying. He was holding one of his squad mate's bodies in his arms, his family, his brother. *I trained him up.* He thought. *He was my responsibility.* That feeling returned to him, the same one that gave him the strength to slay his first monster before he even met the Griffins.

"Solvi." Kieran's voice was a low growl. She stiffened. "Get back to the surface. Order the Hippogriff to sweep for an enemy transport."

"You can't go after them alone." Solvi said.

"I wasn't asking, Private." Jason's limp hand slipped from Kieran's as he stood and gripped his assault rifle. "Get moving."

Kieran looked down a corridor, the one that had the most bullet holes around it, and cast the die. He sprinted towards it, into the yawning shadow, as Solvi called out after him.

But he ignored her. Around the next corner, he saw red, literal red, from one of the enemy's glow sticks.

He was going to kill every last one of them.

## PART 7 - SEEING RED

**AIDEEN KELLY**

Aideen kept her gun trained on the Minotaur at the tunnel's mouth as Isao and Bhanu grabbed weapons from the crates. Howling winds from the jets of the Hippogriff churned dust in billowing swirls around them.

The Minotaur shifted, blowing hot air from its nostrils.

Aideen flinched. "Cap'n, something's happening."

The Minotaur snarled and smashed a muscular ham fist into the wall, crumbling a stone brick.

"Lucas," Bhanu said calmly, "Keep that gun wound."

"Yes, ma'am."

"Sergeant," Bhanu tried the comms, "Kieran, come in . . . Private, Lance Corporal? Bollocks."

Aideen flinched again as the Minotaur surged forward and hesitated at the tunnel mouth. It dragged its hoof against the stone pavers, creating sparks that lit up its ominous bulk from below.

"The artefact's been taken," Aideen said. "Jason," she tried the comms as well, "Jason, come in, dammit!"

The Minotaur roared one final bellow, and it exploded out of the tunnel towards the three Griffins, a pillar of dust following in its wake.

"Christ!" Aideen squeezed the trigger, but she had not yet had a chance to equip herself. Her bullets were useless.

The Gatling gun on the Hippogriff opened fire. A stream of high calibre rounds smashed into the Minotaur, halting its charge in saccade like bursts. But they, too, were not piercing enough for the beast's hide.

"CAPTAIN!" Aideen screamed, looking over her shoulder, but Bhanu and Isao were still loading their weapons.

The Minotaur barrelled towards them . . .

## KIERAN AHMAD

Kieran galloped through the tunnels like the mad beast itself, following the dying light of red glow sticks left in the interloper's wake.

*They killed my squad mate, they killed Jason.*

The thought drove him onwards, a high accelerant fuel to the fire. His pace quickened; his rage broiled over. A heat spread throughout his whole nervous system like searing lightning, supercharging his anger.

They killed Jason, and I wasn't there to protect him!

He rounded a corner, finding a broken wall in the ruins and the odd glint of moonlight beyond. Figures moved in the light.

He barrelled through the narrow opening, scraping his armour and helmet against confining walls without breaking stride, and found himself on a rocky outcropping at the foot of the cliffs by the coast.

Waves crashed into the rocks, breaking over the edges with a deep rumbling and cascading over the small, rounded aircraft that was nestled amongst the terrain. A stealth VTOL craft.

Its side door was rolled open, revealing red night lighting and a team of gunmen loading onto it. One of them carried the dark gold artefact. It pulsed blue with every crashing wave.

"YOU BASTARDS!" Kieran opened fire as he stormed towards the craft.

Two soldiers went down in the barrage; the one with the artefact took cover behind the fuselage. Another turned to fire, but he too was downed by Kieran's rampage.

He dashed over a rock and slid around the base of the craft. Rage consumed him, the pounding sea and spray of salt ebbing from his awareness as he *smelled* blood.

The craft's engines roared to life, but Kieran was already pulling out a C4 pack to slap onto the fuselage.

The gunman with the artefact stepped out from cover and brandished the dark gold prong. It flashed with blue in his hands. At his beckon, the sea surged and smashed into the rocks with a tidal vengeance.

A jet stream of water parted around the craft and the gunman, and smashed into Kieran—and his bomb. He was launched into the cliff face with such force the stone chipped beneath him, his armour cracked and the wind was knocked from him. As the waters receded, he slammed against the ground and the C4 was pulled from his grasp in the current.

With a desperate, gasping wheeze as the wind returned to him, Kieran reached through the hissing foam that slinked back to the ocean. He pawed with white spots in his vision, trying to find the explosive.

The stealth craft alighted from the ground, and the man with the artefact slammed the side door closed. It sped off over the rough seas. The raging waves quieted for the passage of the craft, using the power of they had stolen.

The C4 was primed with a timer, but Kieran had no idea where it ended up. He accepted his fate, collapsing face down in the half flooded rocky terrain. As he drifted out of consciousness, his insides bruised from being smashed by the power of the sea, he waited for the end.

The explosion was closer than he would have liked, and he was buried in rubble.

## LUCAS DEANS

Lucas realised his weapon was useless. The Minotaur powered through the stream of high calibre bullets like it was walking into a leaf blower. There was nothing he could do to stop it from mauling the Griffins on the ground.

"Mon, I cannae stop it!" he cried.

"Roger!" Mon gripped the stick in her hands, and she jammed it hard to one side.

"Mon, what are you doing?" Lucas's stream of fire went wide, tearing a line of destruction across the cracked tiles and up the walls of the dig site.

Mon dipped and swerved the Hippogriff between the Griffins and the Minotaur.

The craft rocked with a deafening shriek as the fuselage smashed into the ground, creating a protective barrier. Mon and Lucas jolted in their chairs, strapped in place as the thrusters whined and petered out.

The Hippogriff was crashed, half on its side with the cockpit exposed to the . . .

A split second later, the Minotaur rammed into them.

Its horns punched through the reinforced glass, pushing the Hippogriff around and penetrating Mon's side.

She cried out in agony as her gut was gored.

"MON!" Lucas pulled out his sidearm and shot through the unbroken glass around the horn breach until it cracked and shattered. Then he emptied his clip into the creature's head.

The beast cried out in anger and pulled back, ripping its horn out of Mon. She cried out again, weaker this time, and went into spasms with blood pouring from her flight suit.

"Mon!" Lucas cried again. He unstrapped himself and rushed awkwardly in the listing cockpit to put pressure on the wound. "You crazy lass, why did you do that?"

Mon coughed as he took off her helmet, blood pouring from her mouth. "My friends were in danger . . ." she drifted out of consciousness as Lucas fumbled for a med-pack.

## AIDEEN KELLY

First, her death was bearing down upon her, and next thing Aideen knew, Bhanu was pulling her back as the entire Hippogriff smashed down in front of them. It wrecked itself upon the ground, and a split-second later, it was smashed further towards them as the Minotaur rammed it.

The ship was pushed back by the force of the creature, smashing into the cargo drop as the three Griffins scattered out of the way.

"Aideen," Bhanu kicked a shotgun towards her, "Armour piercing. Isao's concussed. Get to work!"

Aideen took the weapon in her hands as it clattered to a halt, and the screams of Lucas—accompanied by the sound of gunfire and snarling—brought her back into the moment.

"Engaging!" she cried.

Aideen stumbled to her feet and charged around the crashed Hippogriff's cockpit. The Minotaur was pulling itself from the glass as Lucas emptied his gun into it, and Aiden pumped the fore-end on the shotgun.

She shot it in the face.

It bellowed gutturally as the side of its face was torn to shreds. Its horn was chipped and cracked at the base and it stumbled backwards.

Aideen pumped the shotgun and fired again, and again, as she stalked forward with every shot. She pilfered the Minotaur with armour piercing shotgun shells which tore through its thick hide, shattered its bones, and shredded its organs.

It wailed and bleated like a pig.

Bhanu dashed around the other side of the crashed Hippogriff, an assault rifle at the ready. She fired two short bursts, and the Minotaur stumbled onto its side. Bhanu dashed in to get a killing blow, but it tore a chunk of stone from the ground and lobbed it at her, smashing her gun aside and flooring her.

With panic rising in her again, Aideen pumped and fired the shotgun, only to be met with a horrible *click.*

"Sod it."

Aideen launched forward as the Minotaur picked itself up in a bloody, shredded mess and turned on her. With a snarl, it swung its giant fist to crush her skull. Aideen rolled under the blow and came up drawing her knife.

The Minotaur growled and tried to gore her with its horns. Aideen leaped back, deflecting the cracked horn with her knife. It shattered at the break and fell from the beast's crown. It reared again, trying to disembowel her with the other horn, and Aideen rolled underneath that blow too. She jabbed her knife into the wound on its knee.

It howled in pain and crumbled into a slump. Aideen acted quickly. She grabbed it by its good horn and swung up onto its back. She steadied herself, raised her knife, and jammed it into the crack in its skull by the shattered horn.

The beast exhaled one last snort and collapsed with her on top.

"I'm sorry, beastie," Aideen sighed, pulling her knife from its brain with a squelch, "Wasn't your choice we had to come here . . . Cap'n?"

"I'm good," Bhanu groaned, the sound of someone who was winded. "I just don't feel good. Isao, Lucas, Mon?"

"I'm up, ma'am," Isao's dazed voice drifted over the Hippogriff.

"Mon's down," Lucas's voice was in a panic. "She got gored. We need a medivac now."

"On it," despite the pain she was clearly in, Aideen marvelled at how Bhanu was already on her feet and moving to the broken cockpit. She typed on her wrist pad, "Distress signal sent."

"What about the other fire team?" Aideen slipped off the dead creature.

As she spoke, a panicked voice came in over the comms. "Come in, come in! This is Solvi. We have a Griffin down. I repeat, Griffin down, Kieran is hunting the contacts. The sergeant needs the Hippogriff to scan for escape . . ." Solvi halted in the tunnel, seeing the downed craft, ". . . No."

"Jason!" Aideen screamed and sprinted past Solvi, disappearing into the labyrinth.

# PART 8 – CLASSIFIED

## KIERAN AHMAD

Darkness, grogginess, and an incessant, annoying beep.

Then there was a pale white light, fuzzy . . . Kieran woke up in a hospital bed.

"You're lucky, Griffin." It was an African sounding voice, which didn't give Kieran any clues as to where he was. If he was in a Griffin hospital, it was an internationally sourced branch just like all other Global Response branches.

"I disagree, sir."

"How do you know what rank I am?"

"Because you sound like an asshole." Kieran's eyes adjusted to the light. He could eventually make out a tall Griffin with dark black skin and a small hospital room. Bhanu was sitting to one side. She looked worse for wear. "A major asshole, sir."

The stern face regarded him. "I'm sorry about the losses your team suffered."

"Losses?" Kieran sat up despite the pain and addressed Bhanu. "Who else?"

"Your pilot," the Major continued, "Mon Berger, she was heavily wounded in the fight against the Minotaur. And there were some minor injuries shared by the rest of your squadron. It looks like it got the best of you."

"No sir, there were . . ." Kieran's voice drifted off as Bhanu stood and approached the bed.

She looked pained in more ways than one. "Kieran, it's good to see you awake. The doctors say you should make a full recovery."

"What's happening, Everly?"

She sighed, "It seems the Major here knew about the potential phantom ops element in our scope of operations, and we're not the first team to encounter them."

"Then why not . . ."

"Because," the Major interrupted him, "It's classified, need to know, and *you* don't need to know. That Oxford team unearthed what is believed to be a fragment of Poseidon's trident. There would be many interested parties, that is, if they could get past the Minotaur. It is imperative, Sergeant Ahmad, that the wider Griffin community remains ignorant of these . . . elements."

"Jason wasn't killed by a Minotaur."

"I don't like this anymore than you do, Sergeant." Bhanu said. "But if we don't comply, well, we'll be deemed unfit for service pending a psychological evaluation. *Apparently,* it's too unbelievable for our organisation that there are other paranormal ops out there. Even if knowing about them would . . ." Bhanu took a breath to calm herself, then decided against it. "No. screw that, and screw you, Major. I lost a good Griffin because of this shit. Not just a Griffin, but a member of *my* squadron, *my* family. You've got *a lot* to answer for."

The major raised an eyebrow. "Captain, tread carefully, think of your team."

"Don't get me wrong, Major. As much as I want to break your spine, I'll stick by your stupid cover story for the sake of my surviving squadron, but you need to make it right. And you need to know, informally sir, that this is *beyond* messed up. My confidence in High Command is shaken."

"You will comply, though." The Major said.

It wasn't a question.

"No," Kieran reached for Bhanu's side arm, drew it, and took aim at the Major. "Griffins don't comply with bullshit. I need to know *why.*"

The major regarded Bhanu, "Are you going to let your sergeant get away with this, Captain?"

Bhanu placed a hand on Kieran's weapon. "Sergeant, if you're going to draw a weapon on a major," she flicked a switch on the side, "Make sure the safety is off."

"Sorry, ma'am, won't happen again, ma'am." Kieran said, seething.

The Major raised his hands diplomatically. "Very well, Griffins. I suppose you deserve a bone. There is a shadow organisation out there hunting for relics. We have our theories about what's happening, and what they may need the trident fragment for. But until we know more, until we know the extent of the operation . . . well, *anyone* can be in on it. If they know we know, what hope do we have against further incursions?"

"What hope did we have against the last one?" Kieran growled. "Mon's heavily wounded, Jason's dead, the team is in shambles, and you want to pin it on us? You want to risk all future ops on some piss-weak bullshit?"

"Lance Corporal Jason Armstrong will be given the highest honours as a Griffin. And Monica Berger was flown via emergency orbital-vac to the Spire to receive the best medical care available to humanity. You're due there once you discharge to meet your squadron's replacements."

"Replacements!" Kieran spat.

"We'll need you at full strength for the future conflicts to come. You're Griffins. I expect you to make this work. Now, can I trust you to compl . . ." the Major hesitated. "Can I trust you, for the good of our greater mission, to keep your team in line with this cover up? For the good of all Griffins, for the good of safeguarding humanity against the howling darkness? I promise you; we have more resources than you know working this problem."

"Are these resources gleaning anything from the bodies the phantom ops left behind?"

The Major shrugged. "No identifying marks or documents on them or on their equipment. Sergeant, these are well funded enemies. We need your cooperation in dealing with them."

Kieran sighed, and lowered the pistol, "Aideen isn't going to like this."

"I know." Bhanu said. "But we'll have each other to get through this."

"I will leave you to recover, Sergeant. The doctors expect to discharge you shortly, then you and the rest of your squadron will ship to the Spire to get a new Hippogriff and select your two new members."

"So, Mon is out for a while then?" Kieran said.

"She got gored, Kieran." Bhanu sighed, "Saving Aideen, Isao and I. She's lucky to be alive."

"She's a tough bastard."

"I'll leave you to it." The Major turned and strode from the room.

The Griffins: Bhanu, Kieran, Isao, Solvi, Aideen, and Lucas were in the hold of a transport ship that rattled through the atmosphere on their way to the Orbital Spire.

"I won't do it." Aideen seethed. "Jason deserves better than this."

"We all do." Solvi crossed her arms.

"Don't let his death be in vain." Bhanu said, "If we're pulled from duty over this, the Griffins lose operatives who now have this experience. We'll be more on guard next time."

"What good is that? Jason is dead!" Aideen stormed away.

"Kieran," Bhanu said, "Please."

Kieran limped after Aideen, who moved to a secluded part of the transport ship behind the storage racks. She was crying.

"Kieran, I don't know, I can't, I . . ." She buried her face in his chest and they held each other as she sobbed.

He fought back the tears as well. Aideen was like his sister, the same as Jason was like his brother. He could not bear to see her like this.

"I know you were close to him, Aideen. This is going to be harder for you than the rest of us. But together, we can heal."

"Just the thought of him fighting them off all alone in that place. And now we have to pretend he didn't die that way, it's just . . . Kieran, thank you, for being with him in the end."

"I only wish I was there earlier."

"Then you'd be dead too. After I found Jason's body, I lost it. I was so distraught I didn't even realise I was already charging through the labyrinth searching for you, praying to God that I found you on time. When I came back to my senses, I was digging you out of that rubble and nearly stopped in case I found your body. I can't lose you too."

"You didn't, you won't." Kieran held her close. "You will see him again, Aideen, inshallah."

She nodded and pulled back, wiping away her tears. "I'm getting comforted by an infidel!" She half laughed, "Who woulda thought?"

"Don't tease me, I'm a minority." He chuckled with her. "And *you're* the infidel."

They dealt with their grief in their own weird way, returning to the group and exchanging nods with Bhanu as she went over their next steps.

First a brief recovery stint on the Spire, with as many visits to Mon as she would allow before yelling at them. And then after that, training with the next run of recruits to see who would be the next Griffins in their squad.

And quietly, they would prepare for the real war, the one being fought in the shadows while they fought the monsters of myth and legend.


## THE STORY CONTINUES IN "WEREWOLVES IN SPACE"

# A NOTE FROM THE AUTHOR

Thanks for reading Solar Rain & Minotaur Strike Force!

**Your review would make my day!** An honest review on Amazon or Goodreads helps other readers find this story, and keeps me writing books for amazing readers like you.

**Want more?**

If you enjoyed the bonus short story included at the end of this book **"Minotaur Strike Force"**, you could continue the story in **"Werewolves In Space"** available now!

Visit **SEANMTS.COM** to:

— **Get a free eBook (and audio stories) when you join the community newsletter**
— **Read free short stories and articles**
— **Discover more books you might love**

Stay in contact on Instagram: @seanmtshanahan
Email: sean@seanmts.com

If you enjoyed this story, you will love my other books. You can find an up to date list on my site.

Thanks again.
Take care,
Sean

# ABOUT THE AUTHOR

Sean M. T. Shanahan is a Science Fiction and Fantasy author from Sydney, Australia. He is known for writing emotionally gripping, high-stakes stories that blend dynamic characters with intriguing concepts and take you through darkness into the light.

He has a lifelong passion for storytelling, and since publishing his first book in 2021 has produced multiple books that span Fantasy, Steampunk, Sci-Fi, and children's fiction.

Drawing inspiration from history, science, mythology, and adventure, he weaves immersive tales that will pull you in from the start and leave you wanting more.

Besides reading and writing, Sean enjoys nature, gaming, parkour, endurance sports, and making terrible jokes.